Sharpe's Christmas

TWO SHORT STORIES BY

Bernard Cornwell

First published, 2003, by the Sharpe Appreciation Society

THE SHARPE APPRECIATION SOCIETY

PO Box 14
Lowdham
Notts, NG14 7HU
United Kingdom

PO Box 168
West Chatham
MA, 02669
USA

www.southessex.co.uk

Printed and bound in Canada by Webcom Limited
Design: GarryGatesDesigns

ISBN 0-9722220-1-4

INTRODUCTION

Sharpe's Christmas contains two stories, both written for the *Daily Mail* who needed to fill their pages over two successive holiday seasons. American readers should understand that British newspapers regard the whole of Christmas week as a vacation. Some news will make its way into the paper, but most of the staff will be at home, filling themselves with turkey, stuffing, plum pudding and brandy, and so the pages must be filled with something else. The *Daily Mail* was very specific; each year they wanted a story of 12,000 words, neatly divided into three, so they could run 4,000 words each day, and I took immense pride in delivering that requirement to a tolerance of plus or minus two words. Both stories are now much longer because, free of the restraints, I have taken the chance to rewrite them.

Even at the time the request seemed a bit odd to me. Sharpe, bless him, is not a man of peace. Goodwill? Yes, to those he likes, but he and Christmas are not a natural fit. It is a season, after all, when we enjoin peace on earth, it is about shepherds and babies, angels and wonder, gifts and feasting, while Sharpe is about struggle. The mismatch is almost total, but I was intrigued by the request and tried to write two tales which, while not ignoring Sharpe's belligerent nature, nevertheless acknowledged the Christmas spirit.

For those who like to know where these stories fit into the larger scheme of Sharpe's career, *Sharpe's Christmas* falls after *Sharpe's Regiment*. It is set in 1813, towards the end of the Peninsular War, but the story was written shortly after I had finished *Sharpe's Tiger*, which tells of the Mysore War in India in 1799. Many of the references in *Sharpe's Christmas* hark back to the events of 1799 when Sharpe briefly (and with official blessing) served in the small French force that was attempting to repel the British attack on Seringapatam, and one of the pleasures of writing it was to reintroduce Colonel Gudin, the Frenchman who was one of the first officers to spot the young Richard Sharpe's potential.

The second story, *Sharpe's Ransom*, comes after *Sharpe's Waterloo* and is, therefore, set in peacetime (though Sharpe's life, it must be said, is rarely peaceful). I am often asked what happened to Sharpe after the wars, and whether he really did settle down in Normandy, and so this story provides a glimpse of that new life. I never expected Sharpe to end up in France, but characters often take on a life of their own and, once he had met Lucille Castineau (in *Sharpe's Revenge*), he was not going to lose her, and so to France he went and, as far as I know, stayed there.

I am most grateful to CeCe Motz, my irreplaceable assistant, who had the tiresome task of converting old newspaper pages into computer files so I could rewrite them. And I am also grateful to the *Daily Mail*, ever a lively newspaper, who commissioned the tales in the first place. These rewritten stories are being published by the Sharpe Appreciation Society and the proceeds will contribute to the society and to the Bernard and Judy Cornwell Foundation. The Sharpe Appreciation Society exists, not just to celebrate Richard Sharpe's adventures, but also to increase awareness of the soldiers who fought through Portugal, Spain and France in the early nineteenth century and we hope that the funds raised will help underwrite the society's newsletter and its many visits to battlefields and museums. More information can be found at www.southessex.co.uk. The Bernard and Judy Cornwell Foundation is a charity that concentrates on scholarships for young people in Cape Cod.

Sharpe's Christmas

The two soldiers crouched at the edge of the field. One of them, a dark-haired man with a scarred face and hard eyes, eased back the cock of his rifle, aimed the weapon, but then, after a few seconds, lowered the gun. "Too far away," he said softly.

The second man was even taller than the first and, like his companion, wore the faded green jacket of the 95th Rifles, but instead of a Baker rifle he carried a curious volley gun of seven barrels, each of half-inch bore and fired by a single flintlock. It was a murderous weapon, with a kick like an angry mule, but the man looked strong enough to use it. "No good trying with this," he whispered, hefting the huge gun. "Only works at close range."

"If we get too close they'll run," the first man suggested.

"Where can they run to?" the second man asked. His accent was of Ulster. "It's a field, so it is. They can't run away!"

"So we just walk up and shoot him?"

"Unless you want to strangle the sod, sir. Shooting's quicker."

Major Richard Sharpe lowered his rifle's flint. "Come on, then," he said, and the two men stood and walked gingerly towards the three bullocks. "You think they'll charge us, Pat?" Sharpe asked.

"They're gelded, sir!" Sergeant-Major Patrick Harper offered. "Got about as much spunk as three blind mice."

"They look dangerous to me," Sharpe said. "They've got horns."

"But they're missing their other equipment, sir," Harper said. "They can't sing the low notes, if you follow me." He pointed to one of the bullocks. "He's got some rare fine fat on him, sir. He'll roast just lovely."

The chosen bullock, unaware of its fate, watched the two men. "I can't just shoot it!" Sharpe protested.

"You bayoneted all those goats in Portugal, sir," Harper pointed out, remembering a time when they had been stripping the countryside bare in front of a French advance, "so what's different?"

"I hate goats."

"But this is Christmas dinner, sir," Harper encouraged his commanding officer. "Proper roast beef, sir, plum pudding and wine. We've got the plums and we've got the wine, so all we need is the beef and the suet."

"Where do you get suet?"

"Off the bullock, of course," Harper said with all the scorn of a country-raised man talking to someone from the city. "It's white and tasty, sir, and stacked around the kidneys, so it is, but you'd best shoot the poor beast first. It's kinder."

Sharpe walked closer to the animal. It had large brown sad eyes that watched Sharpe with an expression of gentle fatalism. Sharpe cocked the rifle and the bullock blinked at the strange noise. Sharpe began to raise the weapon, then lowered it again. "I can't do it, Pat."

"One shot, sir. Imagine it's a Frenchman."

Sharpe lifted the rifle, cocked it and aimed straight between the bullock's eyes. The animal still gazed at him. "You do it," Sharpe said to Harper, lowering the gun.

"With this?" Harper held up the volley gun. "I'll blow its bloody head off!"

"We don't want its head, do we?" Sharpe said. "Just its rumps and suet. So go on, do it."

"It's not very accurate, sir, not a volley gun. It's grand for killing Frogs, so it is, but not for slaughtering cattle. And I like the brains, I do. My ma used to fry them in a bit of butter and it tasted lovely. I don't want to spatter brains across half of Spain. Best use your rifle."

"So have the rifle," Sharpe said, offering the weapon.

Harper gazed at the rifle for a second, but did not take it. "The thing is, sir," the huge Irishman said, "that I drank a drop too much last night. My hands are shaky, see? Best that you do it, sir."

Sharpe hesitated. The Light Company had set their hearts on a proper Christmas dinner: bloody roast beef, gravy thick enough to choke a rat and a brandy-soaked pudding clogged with plums and suet. "It's daft, isn't it?" he said. "I wouldn't think twice if it was a Frog. It's only a bloody cow."

"It's a bullock, sir."

"What's the difference?"

"You can't milk this one, sir."

"Right," Sharpe said, and aimed the rifle again. "Just hold still," he ordered the bullock, then crept a half pace closer so that the gun's blackened muzzle was only a few inches from the coarse black hair between the beast's sad eyes. "I shot a tiger once," he said.

"Did you now, sir?" Harper said, without showing much interest. "So just imagine that beast is a tiger and shoot it."

Sharpe gazed into the beast's eyes. He had put wounded horses out of their misery and had shot enough hares, rabbits and foxes in his time, but somehow he could not squeeze the trigger, and then he was saved from having to shoot at all because a small, high and eager voice hailed him from the field's far side. "Mister Sharpe, sir! Mister Sharpe!"

Sharpe lowered the rifle's cock, then turned to see Ensign Charles Nicholls running over the grass. Nicholls had only just arrived in Spain and went everywhere at a tumultuous pace as if he feared the war might get away from him. "Slow down, Mister Nicholls," Sharpe said.

"Yes, sir, I will, sir," Ensign Nicholls said, not slowing his pace at all. "It's Colonel Hogan, sir," he said as he reached Sharpe, "he wants you, sir. He says it's the Frogs, sir, and he says we've got to stop some Frogs, sir, and it's urgent."

Sharpe slung the rifle on his shoulder. "We'll do this later, Sergeant Major," he said.

"Yes, sir, of course we will."

The bullock watched the men go, then lowered its head to the grass. "Were you going to shoot it, sir?" Nicholls asked excitedly.

"What do you think I was going to do?" Sharpe asked the boy. "Strangle it?"

"I couldn't shoot one, sir," Nicholls admitted. "I'd feel too sorry for it." He gazed at Sharpe and Harper in admiration, and no wonder, for there were no two men in Wellington's army more admired or feared. It had been Sharpe and Harper who had taken the French Eagle at Talavera, who had stormed through the breach of blood at Badajoz and cut the great road at the rout of Vitoria, and Nicholls hardly dared believe he was in their battalion. "You think we're going to fight, sir?" he asked eagerly.

"I hope not," Sharpe said.

"No, sir?" Nicholls sounded disappointed.

"It's Christmas in three days," Sharpe said, "would you want to die at Christmas?"

"I don't suppose I would, sir." Nicholls admitted. The Ensign was seventeen, but looked fourteen. He wore a second-hand uniform coat on which his mother had sewn loops of tarnished gold lace, then turned up the yellow-tipped sleeves so that they did not hang down over his hands. "I was worried," Nicholls had explained to Sharpe when he arrived at the battalion just a week before, "that I would miss the war. Awful bad luck to miss a war."

"Sounds like good luck to me."

"No, sir! A fellow must do his duty," Nicholls had said earnestly, and the Ensign did try very hard to do his duty and was never discouraged when the veterans of the regiment laughed at his eagerness. He was, Sharpe thought, like a puppy. Wet nose, tail up and raring to bare his milk teeth at the enemy. But not at Christmas, Sharpe thought, not at Christmas, and so he hoped Hogan was wrong and that the Frogs were not moving, for Christmas was no time to be killing.

"You probably won't have to fight," Colonel Hogan said, then sneezed violently. He pummelled his nose with a giant red handkerchief, then blew scraps of snuff from the map he had spread on the farmhouse table of his billet. "It could be rumour, Richard, nothing but rumour. Did you murder your bullock now?"

"Never got round to it, sir. And how did you know we were going to shoot one anyway?"

"I am the Peer's Chief of Intelligence," Hogan said grandly, "and I know everything. Or almost everything. What I don't know, Richard, is whether these damned Frogs are going to use the east road or the west, so Wellington insists we have to cover both. Or rather the Spaniards will block the east road, and you and your merry men will guard the west. Here." He stabbed a finger down and Sharpe peered at the map to see a tiny mark close to the French frontier and next to it, in Hogan's extravagant handwriting, the name Irati. "You'll like Irati," Colonel Hogan said. "It's a nothing place, Richard. Hovels and misery, that's all it is and all it ever will be, but that's where you're going for Christmas."

Because maybe the French were going there. Wellington's victory at Vitoria had thrown their armies out of Spain, but a handful of French forts still remained south of the frontier and Hogan's agents had learned that the garrison at Ochagavia was about to attempt an escape back into France. The garrison planned to march at Christmas in the hope that their enemies would be too bloated with beef and wine to fight, but Hogan had got wind of their plans and was now setting his snares on the only two routes that the escaping French could use. One, the eastern road, was by far the easier, for it entered France through a low pass, and Hogan guessed it was that route that the French would choose, but there was a second road, a tight, hard, steep road, and that had to be blocked as well and so the Prince of Wales's Own Volunteers, Sharpe's regiment, would climb into the hills and spend their Christmas at a place of hovels and misery called Irati.

"There're over a thousand men in the fort at Ochagavia," Hogan told Sharpe, "and we don't want Boney to get those men back, Richard. You have to stop them."

"If they use the western road, sir."

"Which they probably won't," Hogan said comfortingly, "but if they do, Richard, stop them. Kill me some Frogs for Christmas. That's why you joined the army, isn't it? To kill Frogs? So go and do it. I want you out of here in an hour."

In truth Richard Sharpe had not joined the army to kill Frogs. He had joined because he was hungry and on the run from the constables, and because once a man had taken the shilling and pulled on the King's coat he was reckoned safe from the law. And so Private Richard Sharpe had joined the 33rd, fought with them in Flanders and in India where, at Assaye, a bloody battlefield between two rivers where a small British army had trounced a vast Indian horde, he had become an officer. That was almost ten years ago now, and he had spent a good many of those years fighting the French in Portugal and Spain. Only now he fought in a dark green coat, for he was a Rifleman, though by an accident of war he now found himself commanding a battalion of redcoats. They had once been called the South Essex, but now they were the Prince of Wales's Own Volunteers, though on this dank, grey morning they were anything but willing. They were comfortable in their Spanish billets, they liked the local girls and none were of a mind to go soldiering in a cold Spanish winter. Sharpe ignored their displeasure. Men did not join the army to be comfortable.

They marched on the hour. Four hundred and twenty-two men swinging east out of the town and down into the valley. It had begun to rain heavily, filling the small ditches that edged the fields and flooding the furrows left in the road by the big guns. No one else in the army was moving, just Sharpe's regiment that was going to plug a gap in the high mountains to stop the French escaping. Not that Sharpe believed he would fight this Christmas. Even Hogan was not certain that the Ochagavia garrison would march, and if they did they would probably choose the eastern road, the main road, so all Sharpe expected was a long march and a cold Christmas. But King George wanted him to be at Irati, so to Irati he would go. And God help the Frogs if they did the same.

Colonel Jean Gudin watched as the tricolour was lowered. The Fort at Ochagavia, that he had commanded for four years, was being abandoned and it hurt. It was another failure, and his life had been nothing but failure.

Even the Fort at Ochagavia was a failure for, as far as Gudin could see, it guarded nothing. True, it dominated a road in the mountains, but the road had never been used to bring supplies from France and so it had never been haunted by the dreaded partisans who harried all the other French garrisons in Spain. Time and again Gudin had pointed this out to his superiors, but somewhere in Paris there was a pin stuck into a map of Spain, and the pin represented the garrison of Ochagavia and no one had been willing to surrender the pinprick until now, when some bureaucrat had suddenly remembered the fort's existence and realised that it held a thousand good men who were needed to defend the homeland.

Those men now made ready for their escape. Three hundred were Gudin's garrison and the others were fugitives who had taken refuge in Ochagavia after the disaster at Vitoria. Some of those refugees were dragoons, but most were infantrymen from the 75th regiment who paraded in the fort's courtyard beneath their Eagle and under the eye of their irascible *chef de battaillon*, Colonel Caillou. Behind the 75th, clustered about two horse-drawn wagons, was a crowd of women and children.

"Those damned women aren't coming with us," Caillou said. He was mounted on a black charger that he curbed beside Gudin's horse. "I thought we agreed to abandon the women."

"I didn't agree," Gudin said curtly.

Caillou snorted, then glared at the shivering women. They were mostly the wives and girlfriends of Gudin's garrison, and between them the ninety women had almost as many children, some of them no more than babes in arms. "They're Spaniards!" he snapped.

"Not all of them," Gudin said, "some are French."

"But French or Spanish," Caillou insisted, "they will slow us down. The essence of success, Gudin, is to march fast. Audacity! Speed! There lies safety. We cannot take women and children."

"If they stay," Gudin said stubbornly, "they will be killed."

"That's war, Gudin, that's war!" Caillou declared. "In war the weak die."

"We are soldiers of France," Gudin said stiffly, "and we do not leave women and children to die. They march with us." Jean Gudin knew that maybe all of them, soldiers, women and children alike, might die because of that decision, but he could not abandon these Spanish women who had found themselves French husbands and given birth to half-French babies. If they were left here then the partisans would find them, they would be called traitors, they would be tortured, and they would die. No, Gudin thought, he could not just leave them. "And Maria is pregnant," he added, nodding towards an ammunition cart on which a woman lay swathed in grey army blankets.

"I don't care if she's the Virgin Mary!" Caillou exploded. "We cannot afford to take women and children!" Caillou saw that his words were having no effect on the grey-haired Colonel Gudin, and the older man's stubbornness inflamed Caillou. "My God, Gudin, no wonder they call you a failure!"

"You go too far, Colonel," Gudin said stiffly. He outranked Caillou, but only by virtue of having been a Colonel longer than the fiery infantryman.

"I go too far?" Caillou spat in derision. "But at least I care more for France than for a pack of snivelling women. If you lose my Eagle, Gudin," he pointed to the tricolor flag beneath its statuette of the eagle, "I will have you shot." It was a small thing, an Eagle, hardly bigger than a man's spread hand, but the gilded bronze birds were granted personally by Napoleon, and each held in its clawed grip the whole honour of France. To lose an Eagle was the greatest disaster a regiment could imagine, for the Emperor's Eagle was France. "Lose it," Caillou said savagely, "and I'll personally command the firing squad that kills you."

Gudin did not bother to reply, but just kicked his horse towards the gate. He felt an immense sadness. Caillou was right, he thought, he was a failure. It had all begun in India, thirteen years before, when he had been a military adviser to the Tippoo Sultan, ruler of Mysore, and Gudin had held such high hopes that, with French help and advice, the Tippoo could defeat the British in southern India, but instead the British had won. The Tippoo's capital, Seringapatam, had fallen, and Gudin had been a prisoner for a year until he was exchanged for a British officer held prisoner by the French. He had returned to France then and thought that his career would revive, but instead it had been one long failure. He had not received one promotion in all those years, but had gone from one misfortune to the next until now he was the commander of a useless fort in a bleak landscape where France was losing a war. And if he could escape successfully? That would be a victory, especially if he could take Caillou's precious Eagle safe across the Pyrenees, but he doubted that even an Eagle was worth the life of so many women and children. And that, he knew all too well, was his handicap. The Emperor would sacrifice a hundred thousand women and children to preserve the glory of France, but Gudin could not do it. He reached the fort's gate and nodded to the Sergeant of the guard. "You can open up," he said, "and once we've left, Sergeant, light the fuses."

"The women, sir?" the Sergeant asked anxiously. "They are coming?"

"They're coming, Pierre. I promised, didn't I?"

The dragoons left first. It was dusk. Gudin planned to march all night in the hope that by dawn he would have left any partisans far behind. Until now he had hardly been aware of the fearsome Spanish *guerilleros*, but those savage men had few French enemies left in Spain and they were now closing on the remaining enemy fortresses like vultures scenting death. Gudin had spread a rumour that he intended to march his garrison to join the beleaguered French troops in the fortress city of Pamplona and he hoped that might keep the partisans away from the roads that led northwards, but he doubted the rumour would work. His best hope lay in marching at night, and God help any of his men or women who could not keep up for they would face a terrible, slow death. Some would be burned alive, some flayed, some...but no, it did not bear thinking about. It was not war as Gudin understood it, it was mere butchery, and what galled Gudin most was that the *guerilleros* were only doing to the French what the French had done to the Spaniards.

The infantry marched through the gate behind their precious Eagle. The women followed. Gudin stayed as the sergeant lit the fuses, then he spurred away from his doomed fort. He paused a half mile up the road and turned to watch as the fire in the fuses burned towards the deep charges set in the fort's magazines. He waited, wondering if the fuses had extinguished themselves, staring at the small fort that had been his home for so long, and then the night blossomed red, and a moment later the sound of the explosions punched through the damp darkness. Flame and smoke boiled above the fort's ramparts as the heavy guns were tumbled from their emplacements. Scraps, trailing sparks like comets, arced across the glacis to start small fires in the winter grass, and then there was just silence and flame. Ochagavia had been gutted. Another failure, Gudin thought, watching the great fire rage.

"If my Eagle is lost," Colonel Caillou had ridden back to join Gudin and was still furious that the women had been allowed to join the column, "I shall blame you, Gudin."

"So pray that the British have not blocked the road," Gudin answered. The fort was a dark mass of stone now in which the fire glowed bloody red.

"It's partisans I worry about, not the British," Caillou sneered. "If the British are on the road, then General Picard will come from behind and they will be squeezed to death."

For that was the plan. General Picard was marching south from St Jean Pied-de-Port. He would climb the French side of the Pyrenees to make sure that the frontier pass was open for Gudin's men and all Gudin needed to do was survive the forty kilometres of tortuous winter road that twisted up from Ochagavia to the pass where General Picard waited.

At a place of misery in the mountains, a place called Irati.

"It's not such a bad place," Sharpe said, and it was true that in the fading evening light Irati had a certain picturesque quality. It was a village of small stone houses, little more than huts, with stone roofs on which moss grew. The houses lay in a sheltered valley at the junction of two high streams and were clustered about a small church and a big tavern, the *Casa Alta*, that provided shelter for any folks travelling the high pass. "Can't see why anyone would want to live here, though," Sharpe added.

"They're mostly shepherds," Captain Peter d'Alembord said.

"Shepherds, eh?" Sharpe said, "that's fitting for Christmas, isn't it? I seem to recollect something about shepherds. Shepherds and wise men, isn't that right?"

"Quite right, sir," d'Alembord said. He could never quite get used to the idea that Sharpe had received no education at all other than being taught to read while he was a prisoner in India and what he had picked up over his years in the army.

"A fellow used to read the Christmas story to us in the foundling home," Sharpe remembered. "A big fat parson, he was, with funny whiskers. Looked a bit like that Sergeant who caught a bellyful of canister at Salamanca. We had to sit and listen, and if we yawned the bugger used to jump off the platform and clout us round the face with the holy book. One minute it was all peace on earth, and the next you were flying across the floor with a thick ear."

"But at least you learned your Bible stories," d'Alembord said.

"I learned how to thieve," Sharpe said cheerfully, "and how to slit a throat and cut a purse. Useful lessons, Dally. As for the Bible stories, I learned most of those in India. I worked with a Scottish Colonel who was a Bible thumper." Sharpe smiled at the memory. He was walking north, climbing the road that led from Irati towards the nearby French frontier. He had already found a place south of the village where his battalion could stop the escaping garrison and now he wanted to be certain that no Frogs were lurking in his rear.

"You liked India?" d'Alembord asked.

"It was a bit hot," Sharpe said, "and the food could turn you inside out quicker than a musket ball, but yes, I liked it. I served under the best colonel I ever had in India."

"The Scotsman?" d'Alembord asked.

"Not McCandless, no." Sharpe laughed. "He was a good fellow, McCandless, but a bit fussy, and his Bible thumping was a bloody bore. No, this man was a Crapaud. It's a long story, Dally, and I don't want to bore you, but

I served with the enemy for a bit in India. On purpose, it was."

"On purpose?" d'Alembord sounded surprised.

"All official," Sharpe said, "and I ended up serving a fellow called Colonel Gudin. He was very good to me, Colonel Gudin. He even wanted me to go back to France with him, and I can't say I wasn't tempted."

"Truly?"

"Gudin was a nice fellow," Sharpe said, "but it was all a long time ago, Dally, a very long time ago," and those words signalled that he would say no more of it. d'Alembord wished Sharpe would tell the whole story of Colonel Gudin, but he knew it was hopeless trying to get reminiscences out of Major Sharpe once he had declared it was all a long time ago. d'Alembord had seen men try to learn how Sharpe had taken the French Eagle at Talavera, but Sharpe would just shrug and say that anyone could have done it, it was just luck really, he had just happened to be there and the thing was looking for a new owner. Like hell, d'Alembord thought. Sharpe was quite simply the best soldier he had ever known or ever would know.

Sharpe stopped at the head of the pass and pulled a telescope from a pocket of his green jacket. The telescope's outer barrel had an ivory cover and an inscribed gold plate that read, in French, "To Joseph, King of Spain and the Indies, from his brother, Napoleon, Emperor of France." Another story that Sharpe would not tell. Now he trained the expensive glass northwards to search the misted slopes across the border. He saw rocks, stunted trees and the glint of a cold stream tumbling from a high place, and beyond the stream a fading succession of mountain peaks. A chill, damp and hard land, he thought, and no place to send soldiers at Christmastime. "Not a Frog to be seen," Sharpe said happily and was about to lower the glass when he saw a movement in a cleft of rock on a distant slope. The road ran through the cleft and he held his breath as he stared at the narrow gap.

"What is it?" d'Alembord asked.

Sharpe did not answer. He just gazed at the split in the grey stone from which an army was suddenly appearing. At least it looked like an army. Rank after rank of infantry trudging northwards in dun grey coats. And they were coming from France. He handed the telescope to d'Alembord. "Tell me what you see, Dally."

d'Alembord aimed the glass, then swore quietly. "I'd guess a whole brigade, sir."

"Coming from the wrong direction, too," Sharpe said. Without the telescope he could not see the distant enemy, but he could guess what they were about. The garrison would be escaping on this road, and the French brigade had been sent to make sure the frontier was open for them. "They'll not make it this far tonight," Sharpe said. The sun had already sunk beneath the western peaks and the night shadows were stretching fast.

"But they'll be here tomorrow," d'Alembord said nervously.

"Aye, tomorrow. Christmas Eve," Sharpe said.

"An awful lot of them," d'Alembord said.

"That's true." Sharpe took back the glass and stared at the approaching French. "No artillery," he said, "no cavalry. Just infantry." He watched through the fading light until he was satisfied that there were no cavalry or cannons approaching. "Puncheons, Dally," he said, "that's what we need. Puncheons."

"Puncheons, sir?" d'Alembord gazed at Sharpe as though the major had gone mad.

"That tavern in Irati, Dally, has to be full of barrels. I want them here tonight, all of them."

Because tomorrow there would be an enemy behind, an enemy in front, a road to hold and a battle to win. At Christmastime.

General Maximilien Picard was a disgruntled man. His brigade was late. He had expected to be at Irati by midday, but his men had marched like a herd of spavined goats and by nightfall they still had one steep-sided valley to cross and another precipitous hill to climb, and so he was forced to bivouac a half-day's march from his destination. The camp was a deep, damp valley, bleak as hell, and he could see that his troops were miserable and that pleased the General. Most of his men were conscripts who needed to be toughened and a night among the cold rocks would help scour the mother's milk from their gullets.

The only fuel for fires was a few stunted trees in the hollows where the winter's first snow lay drifted, but most of the conscripts had no idea how to light a fire from damp, tough wood and so they just suffered. Their only food was the rings of hard baked bread they carried on strings about their necks, but at least the stream offered plenty of clean cold water. "Another fortnight," Picard said, "and it'll be frozen."

"As bad as Russia," Major Santon, his chief of staff, commented.

"Nothing was as bad as Russia," Picard said, though in truth the General had rather enjoyed the Russian campaign. He was among the few men who had done well there, but Picard was a man accustomed to success. Not like Colonel Gudin, whose garrison he now marched to rescue. "He's a useless piece of gristle, Gudin," Picard said.

"I've never met him," Santon said.

"Let's hope you meet him tomorrow, but knowing Gudin he'll mess things up." Picard leaned close to the fire to light his pipe and the flames showed the hard lines on his tanned skin. He sucked smoke, then leaned back. "I knew Gudin way back. He promised well then, but ever since India?" Picard shrugged. "He's unlucky, that's what Gudin is, unlucky, and you know what the Emperor says about luck. It's the only thing a soldier needs, luck."

"Luck can turn," Santon observed.

"Not for Gudin," Picard said. "The man's doomed. He means well, he knows his business, but fate doesn't like him. If the 75th hadn't taken refuge with him, we'd have left him to rot in Spain."

Santon looked towards the dark southern heights that marked the frontier. "Let's hope the British aren't waiting for him up there."

Picard sneered. "Let's hope they are! What will they send? One battalion? Two? You think we can't blast our way through a pair of God-damned battalions?" The thought of fighting made him smile. "We'll put our grenadiers up front and let them shoot some *rosbifs* for breakfast."

"Conscript grenadiers," Santon observed quietly.

Picard growled and looked sour, but Santon was right, of course. You could dress a man in uniform, but that did not make him a soldier, and Picard's men were young, frightened and inexperienced. These were not like the soldiers he had marched into Russia. Those had been real men, hard as iron, but not hard enough for a Russian winter. "The British won't bother us," he said dismissively, "we'll find Irati empty. What's there?"

"Nothing," Santon said, "a few shepherds."

"So it's mutton and shepherd girls for Christmas," Picard said, "a last taste of Spain, eh?" The General smiled in anticipation. Irati might be a miserable hovel on the frontier, but it was an enemy hovel and that meant plunder. And Picard still rather hoped there would be a few *rosbifs* guarding the small village, for he reckoned his conscripts needed a fight. Most were too young to shave and they needed a taste of blood before Wellington's army spilled across the Pyrenees into the fields of France. Give a young soldier the taste of victory, Picard reckoned, and it gave him a hunger for more. That was the trouble with Colonel Gudin, he had become used to defeat, but Picard was a winner. He was a short man, like the Emperor, and just as ruthless; a soldier of France who had led a brigade through the slaughter-snows of Russia and left a trail of dead Cossacks to mark his passing, and in the morning, if any *rosbifs* dared oppose him, he would show them how a veteran of the Russian campaign made war. He would give them a Christmas to remember, a Christmas of blood in a high hard place, for he was General Maximilien Picard, and he did not lose.

"Doesn't seem right, somehow," Sharpe said, "fighting at Christmas."

"Tomorrow's Christmas, sir," Harper said, as if that made today's fight more acceptable.

"If we do fight today," Sharpe said, "keep an eye on young Nicholls. I don't want to lose another Ensign."

"He seems a nice enough wee lad," Harper said, "and I'll make sure he gets home to his mother."

Ensign Nicholls was now standing at the centre of Sharpe's line beneath the regiment's twin colours. The Prince of Wales's Own Volunteers were fifty paces back from the frontier that was marked only by a cairn of stones and just far enough back so that any Frenchman coming from the south could not see them beyond the crest. Behind them, on the Spanish side of the frontier, the pass descended gently towards the village, while in front of the battalion the slope fell steeply away. The road zig-zagged up that slope and the enemy brigade would have a foul time climbing into Sharpe's muskets. "It'll be like shooting rats in a pit," Harper said happily, and so it would, but the enemy brigade could still be a nuisance. Its very presence meant Sharpe had to keep his battalion on the frontier, leaving only a picquet to guard the road south of the village where he expected to see the escaping French garrison. Captain Smith commanded that picquet and he would give Sharpe warning if that garrison came into sight, but what would Sharpe do then? If he marched his men south then the French brigade would climb the slope and take him in the rear, while if he stayed on this high crest the garrison troops would appear in the valley behind him. Either way he would be caught between two larger forces and he just had to hope that the garrison did not come today.

There was still no sign of the French who had camped in the deep valley beyond the frontier. They would be bitterly cold by now. Cold and frightened and damp and unhappy, while Sharpe's men were as comfortable as they could be in this miserable place. All his battalion, except the sentries, had spent the night inside Irati's fire-warmed houses where they had made a decent breakfast from twice-baked bread, sour salt beef and strong tea.

Sharpe stamped his feet and blew on his cold hands. When would the French come? He was not really in any hurry, for the longer they delayed, the more hope he had of keeping them out of the village all day, but he had a soldier's impatience to get the grim business done. Grim, at least, for the French, for Sharpe had set them a trap on the road.

That road twisted down from the frontier into a small hanging combe that overlooked the deeper valley where the French had spent their uncomfortable night and in that higher valley, which the dawn now touched with a grey damp light, there were twenty-one big wine puncheons. The barrels were arranged in seven groups of three, and each group blocked the narrow track up which the French must come.

There were twenty-one barrels and above them, hidden among the rocks, were the sixteen riflemen who, like Sharpe, were now enrolled in the Prince of Wales's Own Volunteers. The French hated riflemen. They did not use the rifle themselves, reckoning that it took too long to load, but Sharpe loved the weapon. It might be slow in battle, but it could kill at five times the range of a smoothbore musket and he had more than once seen a handful of riflemen turn a battle's fate. Sergeant Major Harper was commanding the riflemen in the lower valley and Sharpe knew they would fight with terrible skill.

Sharpe turned and stared south into Spain. He could not see Irati, for the village was well over a mile away and his picquets were a half mile further off still, and he suddenly worried that he would not hear Captain Smith's warning shots. But it was too late to change the arrangements now. So stop worrying, he told himself. No point in fretting what you cannot change.

"Enemy, sir," d'Alembord said softly and Sharpe wheeled back to gaze down the road.

The French had come. Not many yet, just a half company of grenadiers, the elite of the enemy infantry. Sharpe could tell they were grenadiers because they wore high bearskin hats with a yellow grenade badge, though none, he saw through his telescope, flaunted the high red plume on their hats. French grenadiers were very protective of that plume and on campaign they liked to keep it in a leather tube attached to their bayonet sling. It was only brought out for formal parades or to impress women, and they fought without it, just as, curiously, they fought without grenades. Sharpe had only ever seen grenades aboard warships, and no wonder, for they were fiddly to light and, being mostly made of glass, fragile to transport. These grenadiers would fight with muskets and bayonets, but they were up against fifteen rifles and twenty-one wine barrels. "Thirty," he counted the enemy as they appeared, "forty, forty-five, sixty. All grenadiers, Dally."

"Sending their best up front, are they?"

"Seems that way," Sharpe said, still gazing through the captured telescope. The Frenchmen had seen the barrels now and they were puzzled by them. They had stopped and seemed to be arguing amongst themselves. "Got them worried, we have," Sharpe said.

"They'll be hoping it's free wine for Christmas," d'Alembord said.

Some of the French grenadiers stared up the hill, but they could see no enemy for the Prince of Wales's Own Volunteers were well hidden behind the crest and Sharpe and d'Alembord were concealed by the frontier cairn. The enemy still did not advance, but at last an officer, a sword scabbard slim at his side, walked towards the waiting puncheons. "It's his lucky day," Sharpe said.

The grenadiers stayed back as the officer approached the strange obstacle. He was cautious, as any man would be on the Spanish frontier, but the barrels looked innocent enough. He stooped to the nearest, sniffed at the bung, then drew his sword and worked the tip of its blade into the cork plug. He levered the tight bung free then stooped to sniff again. "He's found the wine," Sharpe said.

The officer turned and called to the waiting grenadiers who, assured that only barrels of cheap Spanish *tinto* barred their path, surged forward. More soldiers were appearing over the lower crest now, and they too rushed to join in the unexpected booty. Men stabbed their bayonets at the bungs of the barrels, then tipped them over so the wine poured into their empty canteens. A small crowd gathered round the first three barrels and another group, even larger, went to take possession of the second line of barrels. "For what they are about to receive," Sharpe said.

Two of the barrels in the second group contained nothing but stones. But the third, the middle barrel, held gunpowder from Sharpe's spare ammunition. That powder half filled the puncheon and was mixed with scraps of iron and small sharp stones, while above it, balanced on a stave that Rifleman Hagman had carefully nailed into place, was a coiled strip of burning slow match. None of the grenadiers noticed the small holes that had been drilled into the barrel to feed air to the fire, nor did they see the tiny wisps of smoke sifting from the burning fuse. They just anticipated wine and so they prised out the loosened bung and kicked the barrel over.

For a second Sharpe thought the trap had failed, then suddenly the narrow valley vanished in a cloud of grey-white powder smoke that was pierced with livid flame. The smoke churned in the small combe, hiding the awful carnage made by the explosion. Then, as the damp wind began to carry the powder smoke northwards, the thunder rolled up the slope. The sound was like the slamming of hell's gates, and it was magnified by the echo that beat back from the valley's far side. A half dozen grenadiers were dead. One, gutted to the backbone, was sprawled on the road where a score of other men were bleeding and staggering. Then the sound faded and there was just a strange silence in the hills broken by the screams of the wounded.

"Poor fellows," d'Alembord said, for the smoke was clearing and he could see the bodies scattered on the road, and then the riflemen opened fire.

Sharpe's Riflemen did not miss their mark at that close range. They fired from behind the rocks high on either side of the small valley and first they picked off the surviving officers, then they shot at the sergeants and by the time each Greenjacket had fired two rounds the French had vanished from the small valley. They had fled back over its lip, leaving behind a dozen dead and two score of wounded men.

The battle for Irati had begun.

In one way Colonel Jean Gudin had been untypically lucky, for not one partisan had troubled his column on its dark road north, but in every other way his usual ill fortune had prevailed. First, one of the dragoon horses had stumbled on a frozen rut in the road and broken its leg. By itself it was no great accident and the poor beast was put out of its misery swiftly enough, but in the dark the commotion caused a long delay. The carcass was finally hauled from the road and the column had trudged on, only to have the dragoon vanguard take a wrong turning a few kilometres further on. That, at least, was not Gudin's fault, any more than the injured horse had been his fault, but it was typical of his luck and it was almost dawn by the time the column had turned itself about and found the right track winding up towards the high pass. By then Gudin had surrendered his horse to one of his lieutenants who had a fever and could hardly walk.

Colonel Caillou was fuming at the delay. He had never, he claimed, in all his service as a soldier, seen such ineptitude! A halfwit could do better than Gudin! "We are supposed to be at the pass by midday," he insisted, "and we shall be lucky to be there by nightfall!"

Gudin ignored the Colonel's ranting. There was nothing to be done except press on and be thankful that the *guerilleros* were asleep in their beds. In three days time, Gudin reflected, he would be back at a depot in France. He would be safe. And so long as no British troops waited at the frontier he should save Caillou's Eagle and so spare himself the firing squad.

It was just after dawn that the next accident occurred. The column was dragging two wagons, one carrying the heavily pregnant Maria and the second loaded with what small baggage the garrison had managed to rescue from the fort. The front axle of that second wagon broke, and suddenly the horses were dragging stumps of splintering wood across the rutted road. Gudin sighed. There was nothing for it but to abandon the wagon with all its precious possessions; small things—but the property of men who owned little. He did let his men rifle the baggage to retrieve what they could carry, and all the while Caillou cursed him and said that time was wasting, and Gudin knew that was true, but again it was not his fault. So he rescued what he could, then ordered the vehicle to be shoved off the road. With it went his books, not many, but all of them dear to Gudin, but too heavy to carry. He did manage to salvage his diaries, including the two volumes he had written when he was in India and had believed he could drive the British out of Mysore. But the redcoats had won and nothing had been the same since.

Gudin often thought of India. When he had been there he had often cursed the flies and the heat, but since returning to Europe he had come to regret leaving. He missed the smells, the colour, the mystery. He missed the gaudy panoply of Indian armies marching, he missed the sun and the savagery of the monsoon. Most of all he missed his youthful optimism. In India he had possessed a future, but after it, none. And sometimes, when he was feeling sorry for himself, he blamed it all on one young man whom he had liked, an Englishman called Sharpe. It had been Sharpe who caused that first great defeat, though Gudin had never blamed Sharpe, for he had recognised that Private Richard Sharpe had been a natural soldier. How the Emperor would have loved Sharpe! So much luck!

Now there was another Sharpe, an officer in Spain whose name haunted the French, and Gudin sometimes wondered if it was the same man, though that seemed unlikely, for few British officers came from the ranks and, besides, this Sharpe was a rifleman and Gudin's Sharpe had been a redcoat. Yet sometimes Gudin secretly hoped that it was the same man, for he had liked young Richard Sharpe, though in truth he suspected that young Sharpe was long dead. Not many Europeans survived India. The fever got them if an enemy did not.

Gudin walked on, musing on India and trying to ignore Colonel Caillou's insults. The pregnant girl was in pain and crying, and the garrison surgeon, a fastidious Parisian who had hated serving in the Pyrenees, told Gudin the girl was doomed. "She can't give birth naturally," he asserted, "so it's better just to shoot her now. Her bawling just upsets men."

"That's your medical opinion?" Gudin asked angrily. "Shoot her?'

"Put her out of her misery."

"Why can't she give birth naturally?"

"Because the baby is sideways," the doctor said. "It isn't head first. We dive into the world, Colonel, we don't come sideways."

"So cut her open."

"Here?" The doctor laughed. "And if I cut her, she'll die. And if I don't cut her, she'll die. In these circumstances, Colonel, the best medical instrument is a pistol."

"Just keep her alive as far as Irati," Gudin said tiredly, "and there you can operate."

"If she lives that long," the surgeon muttered, and just then a dull rumble came from the mountains ahead. It sounded like distant thunder, but there were no storm clouds over the peaks and a heartbeat after the rumble had faded the small wind brought the spiteful crackle of musketry.

"You see?" Caillou spurred back down the column with a look of triumph. "There's enemy ahead!"

"We don't know that," Gudin said. "That sound could have come from anywhere."

"They're waiting for us," Caillou said, pointing dramatically towards the hills. "And if we'd abandoned the women, we'd be there already. It's your doing, Gudin! I promise, if my Eagle is lost, the Emperor will know it's your doing."

"You must tell the Emperor whatever you wish," Gudin said in resignation.

"So leave the women here now! Leave them!" Caillou insisted. "March to the guns, Colonel! Get there before dark!"

"I will not leave the women," Gudin said, "I will not leave them. And we shall be at Irati long before nightfall. It is not so far now."

Caillou spat in disgust and spurred ahead. Colonel Gudin sighed and walked on. His heels were blistering, but he would not retrieve his horse for he knew the Lieutenant's need was greater than his. Nor would he abandon his mens' women, and so he just kept going and tried to blot out the awful haunting moans of the pregnant girl. He was not a prayerful man, but as he climbed towards the distant sound of the guns, Colonel Gudin did pray. He prayed that God would send him a victory, just one small victory so that his career would not end in failure or a firing squad. A Christmas miracle, that was all he asked, just one small miracle to set against a lifetime of defeat.

General Maximilien Picard bulled his way through the panicked troops to stand at the mouth of the small valley. He could see the dead grenadiers, the smashed barrels and, beyond them, more barrels waiting in the road. A rifle bullet snapped past his head, but Picard ignored the threat. He was charmed. There was no one alive who could spoil that luck.

"Santon!" he snapped.

"Sir?" Major Santon resisted the urge to crouch.

"One company up here. They are to destroy the barrels with volley fire, you understand?"

"Yes, sir."

"And while they're doing that, send the *voltigeurs* up the slopes." The general pointed to where puffs of grey-white smoke betrayed the position of the Riflemen. He did not know they were riflemen, and if he had known, he might have shown more caution, instead he believed the ambush must have been set by partisans. But whoever it was, they would soon be chased out of their lairs by the French light infantry. "Do it now!" Picard snapped. "We don't have all day." He turned away, and a bullet plucked at his cloak, flicking it out like a banner caught by the wind. Picard turned back, looked to find the newest patch of musket smoke and lifted a finger to it. "Bastards," he said as he walked away, "bastards." Who would now get a lesson for Christmas.

"Bugler!" Sharpe called, and the thirteen-year-old boy came running out of the battalion to stand behind his Major. "Sound the retreat," Sharpe ordered and saw Peter d'Alembord lift a quizzical eyebrow. "Any minute now," Sharpe explained, "the Frogs will send their *voltigeurs* up the valley sides and there's no point in our lads hanging around while they do that. They've done their damage."

The bugler took a deep breath, then blew hard. The call was a triple call of nine notes, the first eight stuttering on one note and the last flying high up the scale. The sound of the bugle echoed from the distant hills and Sharpe, gazing through his telescope, saw the cloaked French general turn back.

"Again, lad," Sharpe told the bugler.

The bugle call was sending two messages. First, it was telling Harper's riflemen to abandon their positions and climb back to the ridge, but it was also telling the French that they faced an enemy more formidable than a handful of partisans. They were facing trained infantry, veteran troops, and when Sharpe was certain that the French general was staring up at the ridge in an effort to catch sight of the bugler, he turned and shouted at the Prince of Wales's Own Volunteers. "'Talion! By the right! Forward"—a pause—"march!"

They stamped forward in perfect order, a line of men two ranks deep beneath their bright colours. To the right was the King's Colour, the flag of Britain fringed with yellow tassels, while to the left was the Regimental Colour, yellow as the sun and blazoned with the names of the battles where the Prince of Wales's Own Volunteers had fought. In its centre was the regimental badge, a chained French Eagle that boasted of the day when Sharpe and Harper, in a bloody valley wreathed in smoke, had taken an enemy colour. "'Talion!" Sharpe shouted as they reached the ridge's crest, "halt! Fix bayonets!"

Sharpe was putting on a display for the French. The enemy had been bloodied, they had been panicked and now they faced a long steep climb up a bare cold hill to where they could see the red coats of Britain and the long glitter of seventeen-inch bayonets.

Ensign Nicholls came to stand by Sharpe. "What are we doing, sir?"

"We're giving the Frogs a formal invitation, Mister Nicholls. Seeing if they're brave enough to come up and dance."

"Will they?"

"I doubt it, lad," Sharpe said, "I doubt it."

"Why not, sir?"

"Because they're about to be given a demonstration, lad, that's why. Sergeant Major?"

"Sir?" Harper acknowledged, breathless from his

climb up the hill.

"Three rounds, Sergeant Major, platoon fire, and I want it fast."

"Yes, sir."

The range was much too great for a smoothbore musket, but Sharpe did not have a mind to kill any more Frenchmen today. He had already killed too many for his liking. Christmas should be peace on earth, not broken bodies on a hard road, so now he would show the French exactly what waited for them at the hill's top. He would show them that they faced veterans who could fire their muskets faster than any other troops on earth. He would show them that to climb the hill was to enter hell and with any luck they would decline his invitation.

"Stand back, Mister Nicholls," Sharpe said, and steered the Ensign back through the waiting ranks. "Now, Sergeant Major!"

Harper ordered the men to remove their bayonets that had only been slotted into place for display and which hampered men loading muskets. "Load!" he called, and the men dropped the musket butts to the ground and tore open cartridges. This was the essential skill: the ability to load a musket fast, and Sharpe had trained his men relentlessly. He counted the seconds in his head and had reached fourteen when Harper called that the battalion was ready.

"Platoon fire!" Sharpe called, "present!" The muskets went up to the mens' shoulders and, to the French in the valley below, it seemed as if the whole redcoat battalion took a quarter turn to the right. "Number four company," Sharpe called, "on your command!"

"Four Company!" Captain Bitten called, "Five Company!" He was the senior captain of the two companies and so commanded both when, as now, they worked together. He paused a heartbeat, "fire!"

The two centre companies fired together. The muskets slammed back into their shoulders and a dirty cloud of powder smoke spat across the crest. No more orders were given, but as soon as the centre companies had fired, the platoons on either side pulled their triggers. Each company was split into two platoons, and each platoon waited for the one inside them to fire before firing themselves, and to the watching French it must have looked as though the smoke was rippling out along the high red line.

But any troops could fire one round in a pretty ripple. What would put fear into the French was the speed with which the second bullet was fired and Sharpe noted with approval that the centre companies were all reloaded before the ripple of musket fire had reached the battalion's outer flanks. Those flanks fired, and within a heartbeat the two inner platoons of the centre companies had fired again, and again the ripple spread outwards as the men in the centre dropped their muskets' heavy butts onto the stony ground and ripped the top from new cartridges with their teeth.

The second staggered volley of musket balls whistled out into the void, and then the third followed without a pause. It had been a marvellous display, the best infantry in the world showing what they did best, and if that promise of slaughter did not give the enemy pause, then nothing would.

But Picard was not a man to heed a warning and Sharpe, watching through the thinning musket smoke, saw that the French were not retreating to the deeper valley. And just then, far to the south, from where the picquet watched the road leading into Spain, a musket fired and Sharpe span round.

And knew the other enemy was coming.

"Captain d'Alembord!" Sharpe shouted.

"Sir?"

"You take over here, Dally," Sharpe said, "and I'll take your horse."

The French brigade was forming a column which could only mean one thing, that they planned to attack straight up the hill, though before advancing their leading rank fired musket volleys at the fifteen remaining barrels that blocked the road. None of the barrels contained gunpowder, for Sharpe had only possessed a limited supply, but the French were not to know that. Their volleys riddled the barrels while their skirmishers climbed the small valley's side to chase away riflemen who had long retreated. It would take an hour, Sharpe reckoned, before the threatening brigade was in a fit state to advance, and when they did, he doubted it would be with much enthusiasm, for the display of musketry had warned them of what waited.

But another thousand Frenchmen were coming from the south in a desperate attempt to escape from Spain, and those men knew they must fight through the pass if they were ever to reach home, and their desperation could make those thousand men far more dangerous than the brigade. Sharpe rode back through the village to where a picquet watched the enemy approaching from the south. "They're still a long way off, sir," Captain Smith reported nervously, worried that he had summoned Sharpe too soon.

"You did the right thing," Sharpe reassured him as he drew out his telescope.

"What's happening back there, sir?" Smith asked.

"We showed the Frogs a trick or two, but they still seem to want a fight. But don't worry, they won't be spending their Christmas here." He could see the approaching French column now. There were mounted dragoons up front, infantry behind, one wagon, no guns and a crowd of women and children. "That's good," Sharpe said quietly.

"Good, sir?" Smith asked.

"They're bringing their women, Captain, and they won't want them hurt, will they? It might even persuade them to surrender." Sharpe paused, his eye caught by a metallic gleam above the infantry's dark shakos. "And they've got an Eagle!" Sharpe said excitedly. "That would make a nice Christmas present for the battalion, wouldn't it? A French Eagle! I could fancy that." He collapsed the glass and wondered how much time he had. The column was still a good two hours' marching away, which should be enough. "Just watch them," he told Smith, then he pulled himself back into d'Alembord's saddle and rode back to the frontier. It was all a question of timing now. If the brigade attacked the hill at the same time as the garrison approached the village, then he was in trouble, but when he was back at the northern ridge he saw to his relief that the enemy had already cleared the road of barrels and that their *voltigeurs* were spreading out on the slope to herald the attack. The job of the *voltigeurs* was to advance in a loose skirmish line and harass the redcoats with musket fire. A good skirmish attack could pick off enemy officers and abrade confidence in the waiting ranks and, to frustrate the French light infantry, Sharpe sent his own skirmishers into battle. "Mister d'Alembord! Light Company out! Pick off those *voltigeurs*."

The Light Company, a mix of riflemen and redcoats with muskets, scattered down the hill and took up positions behind rocks. The men would fight in pairs, one man firing while his companion loaded, and the riflemen would concentrate their bullets on officers and sergeants. They waited until at last the French drummers sounded the *pas de charge* and the *voltigeurs*, already ahead of the column, pressed upwards to dislodge d'Alembord's Light Company. The first rifles fired, and a moment later the muskets joined in to dot the hillside with smoke. The French voltigeurs fired back, but Sharpe's men were sheltered by the boulders and none, so far as Sharpe could see, was hit. A French officer was on his knees, clutching his belly, another was shouting his men up the hill and then he, too, was hit by a bullet.

"Amateurs," Sharpe said caustically. The *voltigeurs* were not forcing home their attack, but trying to stay out of range of the deadly rifles. He stared at the Frenchmen through the glass and reckoned they were nothing but children snatched from a depot and marched to war. It was cruel.

The column was advancing now, pressing close

behind the nervous *voltigeurs*. It looked formidable, but columns always did. This one was twenty files wide and thirty-one ranks deep, a great solid block of men who had been ordered to climb an impossible slope into a gale of fire. It would be murder, not war, but it was the French commander who was doing the murdering.

The column lost its cohesion as it tried to cut across the corners of the zig-zagging road and around the splintered remnants of the barrels. Sergeants and officers shoved the men back into place and the drummers beat them on, pausing every few seconds so the men could give a half hearted war cry, "*Vive l'Empereur*!" The rifles were biting at the column's front rank that had advanced so far up the road that the *voltigeurs* were now running to join its ranks rather than fight the British skirmishers. "Call the Light Company in," Sharpe told his bugler.

d'Alembord, grinning because he knew his men had won the fight of skirmishers against *voltigeurs*, came to stand beside Sharpe. "Not a man touched," he said.

"Tell them they did well," Sharpe said, "then send them back to Captain Smith." If the French dragoons rode ahead of the approaching garrison then the riflemen could pick off the horsemen. "But you stay here," Sharpe added to d'Alembord. "I've got a job for you."

The enemy column was getting close now, little more than a hundred paces away, and Sharpe could see the men were sweating despite the day's cold. They were weary too, and whenever they looked up they saw nothing except a group of officers waiting on the crest. The line of redcoats had pulled back out of sight of the enemy and Sharpe did not plan to bring them forward until the very last moment.

"Cutting it fine, sir?" d'Alembord observed.

"Give it a minute yet," Sharpe said. The drums were loud, rattling energetically, though whenever the drummers paused to let the men shout "*Vive l'Empereur*" the response was feeble. These men were winded, weary and wary. And only fifty paces away.

"'Talion! Advance!" The Prince of Wales's Own Volunteers marched forward, their muskets loaded, and Sharpe stepped back through the ranks and tried not to feel sorry for the Frenchmen he was about to kill. They were fools, he thought, fools come to the slaughter.

"'Talion!" Sharpe shouted, "present!"

The muskets came up into shoulders. The French front rank faltered at the sight, then was shoved on by the men behind.

"Fire!" Sharpe shouted and his whole battalion fired in unison so that their bullets smacked home in one lethal blow. "Platoon fire!" Sharpe shouted before the echo of the volley had died away. "From the centre!"

Sharpe could see nothing of the enemy now, for they were hidden behind the thick cloud of grey white powder smoke, but he could imagine the horror. Probably the whole French front rank was dead or dying, and most of the second rank too, and the men behind would be pushing and the men in front would be stumbling on the dead and wounded, and then, just as they were recovering from the first volley, the rolling platoon fire began. "Aim low!" Sharpe shouted. "Aim low!"

A column was a battering ram, designed to let half-trained troops feel the confidence of being part of a crowd, but the men in the centre of the column could not use their muskets for they would only hit their own comrades, while the men in the front ranks and outer files were exposed to the murderous musketry of the redcoat line. That line, only two ranks deep, far outflanked the column and so the musket balls came from in front and from the sides, and the unrelenting fire, the product of endless training, flailed the enemy.

The air filled with the rotten-egg stench of powder smoke. The redcoats' faces were flecked with burning powder scraps, while the paper cartridge wadding, spat out behind each bullet, started small flickering fires in the grass. On and on the volleys went as men fired blindly down into the smoke, pouring death into a small place, and still they loaded and rammed and fired, and Sharpe did not see a single man in his own regiment fall. He did not even hear a French bullet. It was the old story. A French column was being pounded by a British line, and British musketry was crushing the column's head and flanks and flecking its centre with blood.

"They're running, sir! They're running!" Sharpe had posted Ensign Nicholls wide of the line so that he could see past the smoke. "Away and running, sir!" Nicholls shouted excitedly as though he had spotted a fox breaking from a covert. "Running like hell!"

"Cease fire!" Sharpe bellowed. "Cease fire!"

And slowly the smoke cleared to show the horror on the winter grass. Blood and horror and broken men. A column had met a line. Sharpe turned away. "Mister d'Alembord!"

"Sir?"

"Take a white flag and ride to the southern road. Find the garrison commander. Tell him we've broken a French brigade and that we'll break him in exactly the same damned manner if he doesn't surrender."

"Sir, sir! Please, sir!" It was Ensign Nicholls, jumping up and down beside d'Alembord. "Can I go with him, sir? Please, sir. I've never seen a Frog! Not close up, sir."

"They've got tails and horns," d'Alembord said, and smiled when Nicholls looked alarmed.

"If you can borrow a horse," Sharpe told the Ensign, "you can go. But keep your mouth shut. Let Mister d'Alembord do the talking."

"Yes, sir," Nicholls said, and ran happily away while Sharpe turned back to the north. The French had broken and run, and he doubted they would be back, but he was not willing to care for their wounded. He had neither the men nor the supplies to do that, so someone would have to go down to the enemy under a flag of truce and offer them a chance to clear up their own bloody mess. Just in time for Christmas.

Colonel Caillou watched Colonel Gudin walk towards the two red-coated horsemen and felt an immense rage surge inside him. The British were holding a white flag, but only because they would offer Gudin terms and Caillou knew that Gudin would surrender, he knew it, and when that happened Caillou would lose his Eagle that the Emperor himself had presented to the 75th. The standard would be taken back to England and jeered through the streets, and Caillou was determined to prevent that. He drove back his spurs and, in blind fury, galloped after Gudin.

Gudin heard him coming, turned and waved him back, but Caillou ignored him. Instead he drew his pistol. "Go back!" he shouted in English to the two approaching British officers. "Go back!"

"You will leave me to deal with this!" Gudin insisted.

d'Alembord reined in his horse. "Do you command here, *monsieur*?" he asked Caillou in French.

"Go back!" Caillou shouted angrily, ignoring both d'Alembord and Gudin. "We do not accept your flag! You hear me? We do not accept a truce. Go!" He levelled his pistol at the younger officer who held the offending white flag that was nothing more than d'Alembord's handkerchief tied to the ramrod of a musket. "Go back!" Caillou shouted again, then spurred his horse away from Gudin who had tried to place himself between Caillou and the two British officers.

"Sir?" Nicholls looked nervously at d'Alembord.

"It's all right, Charlie," d'Alembord said. "He won't shoot. It's a flag of truce." He looked back to Caillou. "*Monsieur*? I must insist upon knowing if you command here."

"I command here," Gudin asserted with a glare at Caillou.

"Then, *monsieur*," d'Alembord said, removing his hat and bowing in the saddle towards the dishevelled Gudin, "I must tell you that we have already . . ."

"He does not command here!" Caillou shouted, and he pressed a knee against his horse and the animal obediently stepped sideways, knocking Gudin away. "By the authority of the Emperor I am taking command." He turned in the saddle and gestured towards the *voltigeurs* of his regiment who were two hundred yards away. "Advance!" he shouted.

"You do not command here!" Gudin snapped. He was suddenly as angry as Caillou and he drew his own pistol and d'Alembord watched, astonished, as the two Frenchmen threatened to shoot each other, and just then, as their fingers tightened on the triggers, Ensign Nicholl's borrowed horse twitched and the Ensign instinctively reacted by tugging the reins and the horse tossed its head. Colonel Caillou, seeing the motion at the edge of his vision, must have thought the younger British officer was attacking him, or at least trying to disarm him and, still enraged, he swung the pistol round and pulled the trigger.

The pistol's flame was very bright in the dusk. The sound of the shot echoed from the hills, then faded. The *voltigeurs*, obedient to their colonel, were hurrying past the watching dragoons, but then their officer held up his hand.

Because a second shot had sounded.

The shot sounded as Ensign Nicholls was falling from his saddle. Caillou's bullet had torn through one of the gold laces his mother had sewn onto his red jacket and then it had pierced his young heart. He was hurled back in the saddle and the makeshift white flag toppled. He made a choking noise and threw a last fading glance at d'Alembord and then collapsed sideways to thump onto the stony road.

Caillou was suddenly aghast, as if he had only just realised the enormity of his crime. He opened his mouth to speak, but no words came, for Colonel Gudin had fired and that second pistol ball took Caillou beneath the jaw, ripped up through his soft palate and so into his brain and Caillou, without a sound, slumped dead onto his pommel.

Colonel Gudin put his pistol back into its holster. "I command here," he told d'Alembord in English. "To my shame, sir, I command here."

d'Alembord, his face hard as stone, delivered Sharpe's message. One brigade of Frenchmen had already been defeated and the British force at the top of the pass was now ready to give the same treatment to Gudin's men. d'Alembord carefully did not say what forces the British possessed, for if the Frenchman had known it was only a single battalion then he might have chosen to fight. "We are waiting for you with riflemen and redcoats," he said instead, implying that there might be at least two battalions at Irati. "You may fight, sir, or you can spare your mens' lives."

Gudin had heard the terrible musketry and knew what kind of horror his men must endure if they tried to force the pass, but he was not inclined to yield too easily. "I respect your flag of truce," he told d'Alembord, glancing at the red-stained handkerchief that showed beside Nicholl's corpse, "and I agree to talk with your commanding officer."

d'Alembord hesitated. If he agreed with Gudin's proposal then the Frenchman would discover just how weak the British were, but, on the other hand, he would also meet Major Sharpe, and no one had ever thought him weak. So d'Alembord nodded. "You will order your troops to stay where they are," he insisted, "and you may come to the village to discuss terms."

Gudin nodded and the battle, at least for the moment, was over.

Sharpe heard of Nicholls's death while he was still watching the French take their dead from the northern slope. He swore when he heard the news, but he dared not leave the pass, not until he was sure the French brigade was gone, but he sent two more companies back to the village to keep their eyes on the enemy who were waiting a mile southwards. Then, when night fell, and he was satisfied that the northern brigade had withdrawn to the deeper valley and offered no threat, he stalked back to Irati with pure bloody murder in his heart. He saw the horses tethered outside the *Casa Alta* and he kicked open the tavern door in a rage. "What bastard bloody Frenchman dared kill my officer?" he shouted, storming into the room with one hand on the hilt of his heavy cavalry sword.

A tall, grey-haired French officer stood to face him. "The man who murdered your officer is dead, *monsieur*," the Frenchman said in good English. "I shot him."

Sharpe stopped and stared. His hand fell from the sword hilt and his mouth dropped open. For a second he seemed unable to speak, but then he found his voice. "Colonel Gudin?" he asked in amazement.

Gudin smiled. "*Oui, Caporal* Sharpe."

"*Mon Colonel*," Sharpe said and he stepped forward with his hand outstretched, but Gudin ignored the hand and instead clasped Sharpe in both arms and kissed him on both cheeks. d'Alembord, watching, smiled.

"I knew it was you!" Gudin said, his hands still on Sharpe's shoulders. "I'm proud of you, Sharpe. So very proud." There were tears in the Colonel's eyes. "And for your officer who died, I am sorry. There was nothing I could do."

The door from the kitchens opened and Daniel Hagman poked his head through. "Need more towels, Captain," he said to d'Alembord, then noticed Sharpe. "Hello, Major, didn't know you were here."

"Well, I am bloody here," Sharpe said, "and what do you want towels for? Aren't you supposed to be on picquet duty? Not having a bloody bath!"

"I'm delivering a baby, sir," Hagman said, as if that was the most natural thing in the world for a rifleman to be doing on Christmas Eve. "Isn't the first baby I've done, sir. The Frog doctor was going to slice her open, and that would have killed her, but I'll see her right. It's no different from slipping a lamb into the world, except the hooves aren't as sharp. Thank you, sir." He took the proffered rags from d'Alembord and ducked back into the candle-lit kitchen.

Sharpe sat. d'Alembord began to explain that he had permitted the pregnant woman to come to the village, but Sharpe waved the explanation away. He did not care. He saw that d'Alembord and Gudin had started on the wine so he poured himself a mug and took a long drink. "So what am I going to do with you?" he asked his old Colonel.

Gudin spread his hands. "Honour decrees I should fight you, Sharpe."

"Then what the hell are you doing here?" Sharpe demanded truculently.

"You approached me with a flag of truce. I am using that truce to discover what choices I have."

"You've got two choices, Colonel," Sharpe said in a harsh tone. "You can fight me or you can surrender. Either way I don't care. I like a fight."

Gudin smiled. "You haven't changed, have you?"

"Your men are down the road," Sharpe went on as though Gudin had not spoken, "and there's damn all they can do tonight, but you can lead them up here in the dawn. The pass narrows, Colonel, you've seen that, and I'll fillet you. I'll give you a Christmas present of dead men. And don't think your *voltigeurs* can take my flanks. I'll have riflemen up on the hills and they like killing *voltigeurs*. And when they've done for them they'll shoot your officers, then your sergeants, and when your men are a leaderless rabble, I'll bring in the bayonets. I've already done it to those buggers over there," he pointed north, "and do you know how many men I lost?" He paused, but Gudin offered no guess. "None," Sharpe said, "not one. And tomorrow I'll do it again." It was all bluff. If Gudin decided to fight and if Picard renewed his attack in the morning, then Sharpe would be scrambling for his life across the high ground. But when a man held a weak hand it sometimes helped to bid high. "Your choice, Colonel."

"You haven't changed at all," Gudin said. "How many men do you have?"

"Enough."

Gudin looked at d'Alembord. "He took me prisoner in India, Captain, and he was only a corporal then."

"I'm not a corporal now," Sharpe said dangerously.

Gudin smiled sadly. He could see red uniforms and green uniforms inside the tavern and he assumed there were at least two battalions in Irati, and he knew his tired troops could not beat them, and he feared that the partisans might come from his rear in the morning, and so he tugged his sword out of its scabbard and laid it on the table with its hilt towards Sharpe. "I fear I am your prisoner again, *caporal*," he said sadly.

"You and all of your men?" Sharpe asked.

"Of course."

Sharpe hid his relief. He had bluffed and won, so now he pushed the sword back towards the Frenchman. "It's good to see you, Colonel," he said, suddenly friendly again, "it truly is." He poured more wine and pushed the wineskin towards the Colonel. "And how have you been, sir?"

"Not well, Sharpe, not well," Gudin confessed. "You see that I am still a Colonel, just as I was in Seringapatam. It seemed that after that I could do nothing right."

"I'm sure that's not true, sir. You were the best officer I ever had."

Gudin smiled at the compliment. "But I have had no luck, Sharpe, no luck at all."

"So tell me about it, sir. It's the night before Christmas, a good night for a story. So tell me."

So Gudin did.

General Maximilien Picard sulked. He sat by a miserable fire in the deep cold valley and he listened to the moans of his wounded and he knew he had been well beaten. He had scented defeat from the moment he had seen the demonstration volley that the British had flaunted from their high ridge, but Picard had always thought he was a lucky man and he had hoped that his good luck would serve to drive his column up the hill and through the thin British line. But the column had been shattered and his conscripts, instead of tasting victory, were now more fearful than ever.

He drank from a brandy flask. It was three o'clock on Christmas morning, but he could not sleep. The skies had cleared, so that the Christmas stars were bright, but General Picard felt nothing but gloom. "Gudin's doomed," he said to his chief of staff, Major Santon. "If we couldn't break those bastards, what hope does he have?"

"None, sir," Santon said.

"I don't mind losing Gudin," Picard growled, "but why must we lose Caillou? Now there's a soldier for you! And if we lose Caillou, Santon, you know what else we lose?"

"The Eagle, sir."

"The Eagle," Picard said, and flinched. "We will have lost one of the Emperor's Eagles." He said the dread words slowly and his eyes filled with tears. "I do not mind defeat, Santon," he said untruthfully, "but I cannot bear the loss of an Eagle. An Eagle of France, gone to captivity." Santon said nothing, for there was nothing to say. To a soldier of France there was no shame like losing an Eagle, and in the dark hills above them an Eagle was in desperate danger. "I can bear anything," Picard said, "except that."

Then, from above them, all hell broke loose.

To the defeated French brigade in the deep valley it sounded like a battle to end the world. True, there was no artillery firing, but the experienced soldiers claimed they had never heard musketry like it. The volleys were unending, and the crash of those musket blasts was magnified and multiplied by the valley's echoing walls. They could hear faint screams and shouts, and sometimes a bugle call, but above it all, and never ending, the hammer sound of muskets. There was volley after volley, so many that after a while the sound became continuous: a deep, grinding sound like the creak of a hinge on the gates of hell.

"We should go up and help," Picard said, rising to his feet.

"We can't, sir," Santon insisted, and he pointed up to the crest where a line of British soldiers still stood guard. The moon was unsheathed from the clouds, and any Frenchman trying to climb the slope would be a sitting target to those riflemen. "Gudin must fight on his own," Santon said.

And Gudin must have been fighting, for the musketry, instead of fading, grew in intensity. Picard reckoned it must be Caillou who fought, for surely poor old Gudin could never fight a battle like this. Every now and then a brief glow showed in the sky, betraying where a group of muskets flamed together, and soon the heavy foul-smelling smoke spilled over the pass's lip to drift down the moonlit slope. And still the splintering volleys ground on.

Up in the pass Sharpe loaded his rifle. He did it quickly, trained to the intricate motions by a lifetime of soldiering, and when the gun was loaded he raised it to his shoulder, held the muzzle high into the sky, and pulled its trigger. "Faster!" he shouted, "faster!"

And all around him redcoats peppered the sky. They fired volley after volley at the stars, and in between the volleys they whooped and screamed like demons. "I pity any poor angel up there tonight, sir," Sergeant Patrick Harper said to Captain d'Alembord. "He'll lose a few wing feathers, so he will." And then Harper fired his volley gun at the moon and down in the valley the deafened French gasped, thinking that at last the artillery was joining the fight.

"Faster!" Sharpe shouted. "*Vite! Vite!*" A group of French soldiers pulled their triggers, scattering a volley towards the snow on the highest peaks.

Daniel Hagman walked calmly through the chaos and noise. "It's a girl, sir!" he shouted at Colonel Gudin.

"A girl?" Gudin said. "I thought, on Christmas Day, it might be a boy."

"It's a pretty little girl, sir, and she's just fine and so is her mother. The women are looking after her, and she'll be ready to move in a while. Just a little while."

Sharpe had overheard the news and grinned at Gudin. "A cold night to be born, Colonel."

"But she'll live, Sharpe. They'll both live. That's what matters!"

Sharpe fired his rifle at the stars. "I was thinking of the baby Jesus, Colonel. His birth must have been cold as hell."

Gudin smiled. "I think Palestine is a warm country, Sharpe, like India. I doubt the first Christmas was cold. I think Our Lord was born on a warm night."

"But at least he never joined the army, sir. He had more sense." Sharpe rammed another bullet in his rifle, then walked down the boisterous line of soldiers. Redcoats and Frenchmen from Gudin's garrison were mixed together, all of them firing like maniacs into the star-bright sky. "Faster!" Sharpe shouted. "Come on, now! Faster! You're celebrating Christ's birth! Make some bloody effort! *Vite! Vite!*"

It took a half hour before Maria and her newborn child could be laid in the wagon where they were cushioned with blankets and swathed in sheepskins. The new baby had gifts: a rifleman's silver button, a broken ivory boot-hook that a redcoat had lifted from the battlefield of Vitoria and a golden guinea that was a present from Peter d'Alembord.

When the mother and child were comfortable the wagon driver whipped his horses northwards, and all the Spanish women and children whom Gudin had tried so hard to save fell in behind the lumbering vehicle. They climbed the gentle pass, and the French troops who had been shooting at the stars fell in around them as the wagon passed. A hundred Frenchmen joined the women, all of them from Gudin's garrison, and their colonel was the very last man to join the procession. "Here, sir," Sharpe said, and he stepped forward and offered Colonel Gudin the Eagle.

Gudin stared in disbelief at the trophy. "You are giving it to me?"

Sharpe grinned. "I've already captured one, sir, I don't need another. Besides, I took the flag off the staff. Just as a keepsake."

Gudin took the Eagle on its bare staff, then hugged Sharpe and kissed him farewell. "After the war, Sharpe?" he said huskily. "I shall see you after the war?"

"I hope so, sir. I do hope so."

There was one last charade to mount. The riflemen guarding the frontier ridge, those who were in sight of the enemy far below, fired their weapons, then ran in pretended panic as Gudin's small procession approached.

And from the valley below General Picard watched in amazement as a small group of Frenchmen appeared at the ridge's crest. They were only a few men, a mere handful, less than a tenth of those he had expected, but they had fought their way through, they had even brought a wagon through, and then Picard saw a golden glint shine above the dark shapes who fired back at the ridge behind them and he raised his telescope and stared intently, trying to track down the elusive gleam, and suddenly it was there. It was the Eagle. He could see its spread wings. "They've brought the Eagle!" Picard shouted. "They've saved the Eagle!" And his defeated men began to cheer.

The firing in the high pass died slowly to leave a rill of powder smoke sifting down the slope. The riflemen and redcoats grinned. They had enjoyed the nonsense. None had wanted to spend Christmas in this high country that was so far from their beef and plum pudding, but the expedition had turned into a game. It was a pity about Ensign Nicholls, of course, but what had he expected? Everyone knew that Mister Sharpe was fatal for Ensigns, but at least Mister Nicholls was to be buried in France. Sharpe had insisted on that. The boy had come to fight the French and for all eternity he would hold a tiny scrap of captured French soil. But no one else had died. No one else had even taken a wound, and the regiment had turned back a whole French brigade, while in the village, under the guard of the grenadier company, nine hundred French prisoners waited to be marched back into Spain and captivity.

But one hundred Frenchmen went free. One hundred Frenchmen, their women, their children, their colonel and an Eagle. They went free because Sharpe, to help an old friend, had given that friend a victory, and Sharpe now watched Gudin's men go down the slope and he saw the men of the defeated brigade run to greet them. He heard the cheers and in the silver moonlight, framed in the lens of his telescope, he saw the brigade officers cluster around Colonel Gudin. Unlucky Gudin, who on a Christmas morning had saved an Eagle and fought his way to freedom. Colonel Jean Gudin, a hero at last.

"Do you think they'll ever find out that it was all faked?" Harper asked Sharpe.

"Who'd ever believe it? If you heard the tale, would you believe it?"

"I'd think the man telling it was drunk," Harper said, and then, after a pause. "A happy Christmas to you, sir."

"And to you, Patrick."

"I suppose it'll be mutton for dinner?"

"I suppose it will. We'll buy a few sheep and you can kill them."

"Not me, sir. You, sir."

Sharpe laughed, then turned south towards the village. It was Christmas morning, a crisp, clean, new

Christmas morning, and his men were alive, an old friend was a hero and there would be mutton for dinner. It was Sharpe's Christmas.

Sharpe's Ransom

Richard Sharpe tugged off his boots, put both hands in the small of his back, arched his spine and grunted with pain. "I hate bloody cogwheels," he said.

"What is wrong with the bloody cogwheels?" Lucille asked.

"Rusted solid," Sharpe said as he tipped a cat off a kitchen chair. "Sluice gates won't work till the rust is cleared and no one's greased those wheels in years." He groaned as he sat down. "I'll have to chip the things down to bare metal, then clear the leat."

"The leat?" Lucille asked. She was still learning English.

"The channel that takes the water to the mill, love. It's full of rubbish." Sharpe poured himself some red wine. "It'll take me a week to clear that."

"It's Christmas in two days," said Lucille.

"So?"

"So at Christmas you rest," Lucille declared, "and the leat and the sluice gate and the bloody cogwheels can all rest. It *is* a holiday. I shall cook you a goose."

"You cooked my goose long ago, girl," Sharpe said.

Lucille made a dismissive noise, collected a pile of washing from the table and walked down the scullery passage. Sharpe tipped his chair back to watch her, and Lucille, knowing she was being observed, deliberately swayed her hips. "Cooked it proper, you did!" Sharpe called after her.

"If you want supper," she spoke from the washroom at the end of the passage, "the stove needs wood."

Sharpe glanced up as a gust of wind howled at the farm's high gables. A year before, when he had returned to Normandy after the Waterloo campaign, the big gabled roof had leaked and every door and window had let in killing draughts, but he had retiled the roof, mortared the window frames and mended the doors. It had cost a penny or two, and all of it had come from the half-pay Sharpe received as a retired British officer, because the farm was not making any profit. Not yet, anyway, and whether it ever would was dubious.

"Bloody frog taxes," Sharpe grumbled as he tossed wood into the stove. He closed the firebox door, then hung his wet boots from the mantel so they would dry. They could not be placed too near the heat or else the leather would crack, but he had hung his old rifle on the chimneypiece and by dangling one boot from the muzzle and the other from the lock he knew they would be dry by morning. He paused to touch the rifle's stock, remembering.

"You miss it?" Lucille had come back to the kitchen.

"I wasn't thinking about the army," Sharpe said, "but of shooting some foxes tomorrow. Lambing's not far off. Then it's back to that bloody mill. Christmas or not, I've got to chip those wheels, clear the leat, then rebuild the paddles. God knows how long it'll all take."

"In the old days," Lucille said, "we would have the whole village to help, and when the work was done we would give them a feast."

"Those were the good old days," Sharpe said, "and they were too good to last. And it wouldn't do me much bloody good asking the village for help, would it? They'd as soon shoot me as help me."

"You must give them time," Lucille said. "They are peasants. If you live here twenty years they will begin to recognize you."

"Oh, they recognize me well enough," Sharpe said. "Cross the street, they do, so they don't have to breathe the same air as me. It's that bloody Malan. Hates me, he does."

Lucille shrugged. "Poor Jacques is still loyal to Bonaparte," she said. "He liked being in the army. And besides . . ." she hesitated.

"Besides what?" Sharpe prompted her.

"A long time ago, when I was a girl, Jacques Malan thought he was in love with me. He haunted me. One night he was even on the roof!" She sounded indignant at the memory. "He was peering through my bedroom window!"

"Get an eyeful, did he?"

"More than he should have!" said Lucille. "My father was furious that Jacques should even think about me. Jacques Malan was a peasant, and my father was the Vicomte de Seleglise." She laughed. "But Jacques's not such a bad man. Just disappointed."

"He's a lazy bastard, that's what he is," Sharpe said. "I cut that timber for the priest and Jacques was supposed to collect it, but has he? Hell, he does nothing but drink his mother's money away." The thought of Jacques Malan always made Sharpe angry, for Malan seemed determined to drive Sharpe from the village by sheer unfriendliness. The big man had returned defeated from Waterloo and ever since had sat around the village in a sulk. He did no work, he earned no wages, he just sat glowering at the passing world and dreaming of the days when the Emperor's soldiers had strutted through Europe. The rest of the village feared to cross him, for though he had neither land nor money, Jacques Malan possessed an undeniable force of character and was massively strong. "He was a sergeant, wasn't he?" Sharpe asked.

"A sergeant in the Imperial Guard," Lucille confirmed, "the Old Guard, no less."

"And I'm the only enemy he's got left now, so there's not much hope of him helping me clear out the leat. Sod him," Sharpe said. "Is Patrick asleep?"

"Fast asleep," Lucille said, then frowned. "Why do you English say 'fast asleep'? Why not slow asleep? I think your language is mad."

"Fast or slow, who cares? Long as the child's asleep, eh? So what shall we do tonight?"

Lucille skipped away from his arms. "For a start, we shall eat."

"And after that?"

Lucille let herself be caught. "Who knows?" she asked, though she did know, and she closed her eyes and prayed that Sharpe would stay in Normandy, for she worried that the village might yet repel him. A man could not live without friends, and Sharpe's friends were far away, too far away, and she cared for his happiness.

But this was her farm and her ancestral house, and she could not bear the thought of leaving Seleglise. Let us stay, she prayed, please God, make Richard happy here and let us stay.

Sharpe woke early on the morning of Christmas Eve. He slid from the bed, picked up his clothes from the chair beside the door, paused to look at his son who slept in a crib at the foot of the bed, then tip-toed from the room so as not to wake Lucille. He hurried to the kitchen where, still naked, he stooped to riddle the stove and feed it with wood.

"*Bonjour, monsieur*!" Marie, the old woman who was the one house servant left, peered at him from the larder.

"You're up early," Sharpe said, snatching his shirt to hide his nakedness.

"The one who rises early gets to see the best sights," the old woman said, "and dress warm, *monsieur*, there is going to be snow."

"It doesn't snow here," Sharpe said.

"Enough to muffle the devil's footsteps," Marie said gnomically, then closed the larder door to let Sharpe dress.

He dressed very warmly, knowing that the cold outside would be brutal. He took a shotgun and a full powder horn from the cupboard, filled a coat pocket with loose shot, then added cartridges for the rifle. He doubted he would use the rifle, but he liked to carry it in case a deer crossed his path.

He pulled on a woollen hat, unbarred the back door and stepped into the courtyard where the cold hit him like a blast of cannon shot. He pulled open the stable door to let Nosey out. The dog scampered and jumped until Sharpe growled at him to heel and together they crossed the moat that was skimmed with ice. The reeds at the moat's edge were brittle and frost-edged, while a pearly mist hung in the bare trees on the ridge above the farm. The sun was not yet up and the world was still grey with the thin light between night and day, the half light when picquets would imagine movement in the shadows and the camp fires would spread a fog of smoke. Old days, Sharpe thought, old days and gone. The world was at peace and he was a farmer now.

He climbed the ridge, the dog padding behind, and when he reached the top he glanced back and noted that the smoke from the farm's chimneys was drifting east, which meant he would have to make a circuit about the big wood to keep himself upwind of the valley where he know the foxes had their lairs. With any luck he would bag a couple. He hated foxes. A single fox could rip a dozen newborn lambs to death in an eye blink. They had decimated the ducks on the farm's moat and killed a score of Lucille's chickens. No wonder the farm made no money, it was besieged by foxes, and what he should do, Sharpe thought, was dig the beasts out, but to do that he would need a dozen men. Father Defoy would offer to help, and so would the doctor, but neither man was fit for hard physical labour, and Jacques Malan made certain that no one else from the village would ever help the Englishman. Damn Malan, he thought.

It took him the best part of an hour to reach the upwind side of the small valley where he crept to the wood's edge with the shotgun already loaded and rammed. The eastern horizon was now a sullen red and the wind-driven mist drifted across the valley where a score of rabbits fed. No foxes yet.

Sharpe guessed his first intimation of a fox would be the thump of a rabbit's warning feet, then the scamper as they fled to their burrows. A moment or so later he would see the dark fur slinking along the edge of the trees and he would have one chance of a shot. He reckoned he would bag his second fox lower down, but only after his terrier Nosey had flushed it from wherever it had gone to shelter.

It was just like war, he thought. Set an ambush, give the enemy a bloody nose, then attack to finish him off. Except the trouble with bloody foxes was that they never were finished off, but he had to try and so he worked his way up to the wood's edge at the head of the valley from where he could again see the roof of the farmhouse. He called it a farmhouse, but Lucille insisted it was the Chateau Lassan, and the gate to the yard still had a crenellated tower and the buildings were surrounded by a moat, so perhaps she was right. Years before, back when men rode in plate armour, the Vicomtes of Seleglise had lorded over a dozen villages from the Chateau Lassan, but the castle had crumbled and all that was left was a chapel, a barn, the dairy, the stables, the watermill and the big farmhouse where Sharpe had found Lucille.

Lucille and happiness, he thought, except that a man could not live among a people who dismissed him as an enemy, and if the villagers went on rejecting him he knew he would have to go back to England. He did not want that. He did not want to leave Normandy, and he knew Lucille would hate to go from the land that had been in her family for 800 years, but a man could not live among enemies. And what would he do in England, Sharpe wondered. He could not afford any land there, not unless Lucille sold the chateau, and that would break her heart. It would break his heart too, Sharpe thought, for he was learning to love this patch of stubborn Norman earth.

A group of six men appeared on the road above the farm and Sharpe frowned in puzzlement. There was little enough traffic on that road at any time, let alone on a cold winter's dawn, but then he remembered that Marie had forecast snow and he supposed the men must be hurrying to find shelter in the village that lay just beyond the high, tree-lined ridge above the farm and he glanced up to see that the sky was leaden and heavy and he reckoned the old servant was right and they were probably in for a blizzard.

The small group vanished behind black trees and Sharpe waited for them to reappear where the road crossed the stream at the valley's end. They would pass the farm, then climb the northern part of the ridge to go to the village. A cockerel crowed from the Chateau Lassan and Sharpe looked to the east to see that the sun was now a blurred circle behind the storm clouds. There was one small gap far off in the grey and the dawn's red light seeped through the rent like blood leaking through a bandage. He shuddered at the image. He still woke in the nights, shaking with memories of blood and battles, but he consoled himself that it was all behind him now. He had Lucille, he had a son and, given time, he might even find happiness in this land of his erstwhile enemies.

Then a rabbit thumped in warning. Nosey growled softly and Sharpe opened his eyes, slid the gun forward and waited.

L ucille fed Patrick his breakfast. "Almost two years old!" she told the child, tickling under his chin.

"Big for his age," their housekeeper Marie said. "He'll grow up to be a soldier like his father."

"I pray not," Lucille said, crossing herself.

"Where's papa?" Patrick wanted to know.

"Shooting foxes," Lucille said, spooning porridge into her son's mouth.

"Bang," Patrick said, spraying the porridge over the table.

"Patrick Lassan!" Lucille said reprovingly.

"Lassan?" Marie asked, "not Castineau? Not Sharpe?"

"Lassan," Lucille said firmly. Lucille's maiden name had been Lassan, then she had married a cavalry officer called Castineau who had died for France in the horrors of Russia, and now she lived with Sharpe, and the village, who rightly suspected that Lucille and her Englishman were not married, never quite knew whether to call her Mademoiselle Lassan, the widow Castineau or Madame Sharpe. Lucille herself did not care what she was called, but she was determined that her family name would go on to the next generation and so her son, Sharpe's son, was called Patrick Lassan. Sharpe did not mind. "You pick his second name," he had told Lucille, "and I'll choose his first," which was why the boy was named after an Irish sergeant who now ran a tavern in Dublin.

Lucille jumped, startled, as the old bell clanged in the courtyard to announce that someone was at the main gate. "Who would call so early?" Lucille asked.

"The priest?" Marie suggested, taking a shawl from the hook behind the door. "He'll be wanting his firewood." She draped the shawl over her thin shoulders. "And early or not, Madame, he'll want his glass of brandy too." She went into the yard, letting in a gust of freezing air, and Lucille instinctively cuddled Patrick.

"Bang," the boy said again, reckoning that the sight of splattering porridge was worth the risk of a cuff about the ear, but Lucille was too distracted to notice. She was thinking that it was not like Father Defoy to be up so early and an instinct made her put Patrick into his chair and cross to the hearth where she reached for the rifle, then she realised the weapon was gone.

She heard the gate squeal open, there was the mutter of a man's voice and suddenly Marie gave a shout of indignation that was abruptly cut short. Lucille ran to the cupboard where Richard kept his other guns, but before she even had time to turn the key, the kitchen door banged open and a tall man with a face like old scratched leather was standing in the doorway where his breath misted in the cold air.

He slowly raised a pistol so that it was pointing between Lucille's eyes, then, just as slowly, he thumbed the cock back. "Where is the Englishman?" he asked in a calm voice.

Lucille said nothing. She could see there were other men in the yard.

"Where is the Englishman?" the tall man asked again.

"Papa's shooting foxes!" young Patrick explained helpfully. "Bang!"

A small bespectacled man pushed past the man with the pistol. "Look after your child, Madame," he ordered Lucille, then he stepped aside to let his five ragged followers into the kitchen. Patrick, at last sensing that his safe world had gone awry, had begun to cry and the noise made the small man flinch. He was the only one of the strangers who did not carry a pistol, and the only one who did not have long pigtails framing his face. The last man through the door dragged Marie out of the cold and pushed her down onto a chair.

"Who are you?" Lucille demanded of the small man.

"Look after your child, Madame!" the bespectacled man insisted again. "I cannot abide the noise of small children." He unwound a scarf from his neck then warmed his hands by the stove while the tall man who had first appeared in the doorway shepherded Lucille away from the gun cupboard. He looked to be around forty years old, and everything about him declared that he was a soldier from the wars. The pigtails had been the badge of Napoleon's hussars, and they framed a face that had been scarred by blades and stained with powder burns. His coat was an army coat with the bright buttons replaced by horn, while his cap was a forage hat which still had Napoleon's badge. He pushed Lucille into a chair, then turned to the small man. "We'll start the search now, *Maître*?"

"Indeed," the small man said.

"Who are you?" Lucille asked again, this time more

fiercely.

The small man took off his coat, revealing a shabby black suit. "Make sure she stays at the table," he said to one of the men, ignoring Lucille's question, "the rest of you, search! Sergeant, you start upstairs."

"Search for what?" Lucille demanded as the intruders spread out through the house.

The small man turned back to her. "You possess a cart, *Madame*?"

"A cart?" Lucille asked, confused.

"We shall find it, anyway," the man said. He crossed to the window, rubbed mist from a pane and peered out. "Your Englishman is shooting, yes? So when will he return?"

"In his own time," Lucille said defiantly. There was a shout from the old hall where one of the strangers had discovered the remnants of the Lassan silver. There had been a time when a lord of this chateau could seat forty diners in front of silverware, but now there was just a thick ewer, some candlesticks and a dozen dented plates. The silver was brought into the kitchen, where the small man ordered that it be piled beside the back door.

"We are not rich!" Lucille protested. She was trying to hide her fear, thinking that the farm had been invaded by one of the desperate bands of old soldiers who roamed and terrorized rural France. The newspapers had been full of their crimes, yet Lucille had somehow believed that the troubles would never reach Normandy. "That is all we have!" she said, pointing to the silver.

"You have more, *Madame*," the small man said, "much more. And I would advise you not to try to leave the house, or else Corporal Lebecque will shoot you." He nodded to her, then ducked under the staircase door to help the men who were ransacking the bedrooms.

Lucille looked at the thin corporal who had been ordered to watch her. "We are not rich," she said again.

"You're richer than we are," the corporal answered. He had a ferret's face, Lucille thought, with ravaged teeth and sallow eyes and a torn ear behind his left pigtail. The Emperor's hussars had all sported the pigtails that grew from their temples, and the longer the pigtail the longer the service. They were a mark of pride, a display which announced the hussar's elite status, and the fact that six of the invaders sported the old pigtails announced that their allegiance had not changed since the Emperor was exiled to Saint Helena. "You're much richer than we are," he added.

"You won't hurt us?" Lucille asked, clutching Patrick.

"That depends on your Englishman," the corporal said, "and on my sergeant's mercy."

"Your sergeant?" Lucille asked, guessing he meant the big man who had first confronted her.

"And my sergeant," the corporal continued, "does not have mercy. It was bled out of him in the war. It was bled out of us all. You have coffee?"

A shot sounded far away, and Lucille thought of the terrible things that war had left in its wake. She remembered the stories of pillage and murder that racked poor France and which now, at Christmas, had arrived at her own front door. She held her crying child, closed her eyes and prayed.

The fox had twisted in the air when it was hit, a last reflex making the beast leap to escape the shot, and then it fell to leave a smear of blood on the frosted grass.

"One less," Sharpe told Nosey. "Not yet, boy," he said, nudging the dog away from the corpse and he wondered if he should skin it for the fur, then he decided to hell with it and he contented himself by cutting off the brush that he would nail on the barn door. There were a score of other fox brushes on that big door and they were supposed to drive the other foxes away from the Chateau Lassan, but somehow the ancient magic was not working.

He slit the fox's belly open to let Nosey have a feed, then he turned and looked down the valley. Odd, he thought, that the group of pedestrians had not appeared on the road beyond the farm.

The familiar smell of powder smoke lingered as he stared down the valley. Maybe the travellers had been in a hurry and were already hidden by the beech trees on the far slope? But those trees were bare and he could see no flicker of movement where the road climbed beneath their branches.

Damn it, he thought, but they should be in sight, and suddenly the old instinct of danger prickled at him and so he called Nosey to heel, slung the gun on his shoulder and began walking down the valley. He told himself he was being ridiculous. The world was at peace, Christmas was a day away and folk had the right to walk rural roads without sparking the suspicions of a retired rifleman, but Sharpe, like Lucille, read the newspapers.

In Montmorillon, just a month before, a group of ex-soldiers had invaded a lawyer's house, had killed him and his wife, stolen their goods and dragged the daughters away. The two girls, sixteen and fourteen, had been raped repeatedly and then tossed into a pond. The youngest had survived to tell the tale. All across France similar things happened. There was no work, the harvest had been scanty and men back from the wars had no homes, no money and no hope, but they did possess the skills of foraging and plundering that Napoleon had encouraged in his soldiers.

Sharpe was certain now that the travelers had not climbed the road to the village, which meant they had either turned back the way they had come or else gone to the farm. And maybe they had business there? Maybe they were just beggars, for not all the soldiers back from the wars were violent criminals, most just roamed the countryside asking for food. Sharpe had fed enough of them in the last few months and he usually enjoyed those encounters with his old enemies. One such beggar had been on the walls of Badajoz, a Spanish citadel attacked by the

British, and he had boasted how many Englishmen he had killed in the ditch at the foot of the central breach, and Sharpe had never told him he had been in that same ditch, nor that he had climbed the breach in a storm of blood and fire to send the Frenchmen running.

It was over, he told himself, it was over and gone and good riddance to it.

So maybe they were just beggars, he thought, but even so Sharpe did not like leaving Lucille, Marie and Patrick alone with a group of hungry men who might just be tempted to take more than they were offered, and so he forgot the second fox and hurried home, taking the short route, across the shoulder of the hill and down the steep slope to where the choked mill-leat was glazed with ice.

He crossed the leat bridge, something else that needed rebuilding, and stopped to gaze into the farm's courtyard beyond the moat. Nothing moved there.

Smoke drifted from the kitchen chimney. The windows were frosted. Everything looked as it should, and yet the danger still nagged him. It was a feeling he had come to trust, a feeling that had saved his life on countless Spanish fields. He thought about loading the rifle, then decided it was too late. If there were men in the farm then there would be too many for one rifle bullet. Besides, they would already be watching him and it was best not to make a show of hostility.

What would be best, he thought, was to get the hell away from here and watch the farmhouse until he understood if there was danger or not, but he had no choice in the matter because Lucille and his son were inside the farm, and so he had to go there even though his every instinct shrieked at him to stay away. "Come on Nosey," he said, and he walked on, crossing the back bridge over the moat and anticipating what a fool he would feel as he pushed the kitchen door open to discover Lucille feeding Patrick, Marie chopping turnips and the stove blazing cheerfully.

The war had left him nervous, he told himself,

nervous, jumpy, skittish and prone to fears, and it was all nonsense. Nothing was wrong. Tomorrow was Christmas and all was well with the world, except that the world needed rebuilding.

He pushed open the kitchen door. "Got one of the sods," he announced happily, brandishing the fox's brush, then went very still. A small bespectacled man was sitting opposite Lucille while another man was behind her with a pistol pointing at her black hair.

Marie was huddled in the corner chair, while in front of Sharpe, and carrying Sharpe's old sword that he had taken down from the wall above the spice cupboard, was a tall man with hussar pigtails framing a face that was as hard as horn.

"Remember me?" the tall man said. "Because I remember you."

He pushed the sword forward until its point touched Sharpe's neck. "I remember you very well, Major Sharpe," he said, "very well indeed. Welcome home."

S harpe sat beside Lucille at his kitchen table. One man stood behind him with a pistol while Sergeant Guy Challon chopped Sharpe's sword into the table's edge.

"A clumsy weapon," he said derisively.

"It works better on Frenchmen than on tables," Sharpe said mildly.

"Put the sword down, Sergeant!" the small man complained. "Put it on the pile. Someone will pay a few francs for it."

The small man watched as the sergeant added the sword to the pile of silver and other small valuables that was growing beside the kitchen door. The collected loot included Lucille's small stock of jewellery, among which had been a large ruby that had come from Napoleon's own treasure chests and the bespectacled man had seized on the stone as evidence of Sharpe's wealth. He held the stone, gazing at it, revelling in it, and when Sharpe had sat down he held the stone towards the Englishman as though it would prove something. "My name," the small man said, "is *Maître* Henri Lorcet. I am a lawyer who had the honour of drawing up the last will and testament of Major Pierre Ducos. This is it," he said, producing a long document that he smoothed on the kitchen table. He tapped the paper with the ruby as though the will somehow gave legitimacy to his presence.

"The will mentions the existence of a hoard of gold," Lorcet said, glancing up at Sharpe so that the wan light flashed off his round spectacle lenses, "a hoard that was once the property of Napoleon Bonaparte. Major Ducos was kind enough to bequeath the treasure to me and to Sergeant Challon," he nodded to the grim hussar who had been amusing himself with Sharpe's sword, "and Major Ducos further indicated that you would know where the gold was to be found." He paused. "You do know about this gold, Major Sharpe?"

Lucille was about to protest that Lorcet was talking nonsense, but Sharpe laid a hand on her arm. "I know about it," he admitted. Two years before, when Napoleon had been banished to Elba, Sharpe had helped rescue the Emperor's treasure that had been lost on its journey to the island. Pierre Ducos had stolen the gold, and Sergeant Challon had been Ducos's helper, and though Ducos was long dead, he had somehow reached from his grave to wish this trouble on his old enemy.

"But we have nothing!" Lucille insisted, "other than what you see."

Maître Lorcet took no notice of her protest. "The value of the gold," he spoke very calmly and reasonably, "amounted to 200,000 francs, I believe?"

Sharpe laughed. "Your friend Ducos spent half of that!"

"So? 100,000 francs," Lorcet said equably, as well he might, for the halved sum was still close to £50,000, and a man could live in luxury on £200 a year, and with

£50,000 he could live royally.

"I wasn't alone when I took that gold," Sharpe told the lawyer. "Ask your friend, Sergeant Challon." He jerked his head at the big man. "I was with General Calvet. You think he didn't want some of the gold?"

Lorcet looked at Challon who nodded reluctantly. "Calvet was there, *maître*," he confirmed.

The lawyer merely shrugged. "So you divided the treasure," he conceded, "but there must still be a considerable amount remaining."

Sharpe was silent.

"I'll hit him, *maître*," Challon offered.

"I detest violence," the lawyer said with some asperity, "it is the refuge of the incompetent and the stupid. Reason is a better instrument. Be truthful with me, Major," he pleaded with Sharpe, "you have surely not spent it all?"

Sharpe sighed as though surrendering to the inevitable. "There's 40,000 francs left," he confessed, and heard Lucille's gasp of surprise. "Maybe a bit more," he admitted grudgingly.

Henri Lorcet smiled with relief for he had feared there would be nothing at the end of his long quest, and though 40,000 francs was less than he had hoped for it was still a considerable fortune in these hard times. "So tell me where it is, Major," he said, "and we shall take it away and leave you in peace."

It was Sharpe's turn to smile. "It's all in a bank, Lorcet," he said, "all in Monsieur Plaquet's bank in the Rue Deauville in Caen. It's in a big iron-cornered box, locked in a stone vault behind an iron-ribbed door and Monsieur Plaquet has one key to the vault and I have the other."

Sergeant Challon spat at the stove, then twisted and untwisted one of his long pigtails. "He's lying," he growled at the lawyer. "Let me knock the truth out of him."

"So hit me, Sergeant," Sharpe said, "and then tear the chateau down, and when you find nothing, what will you do then?"

"I'll hit you again," Challon suggested, "and take what we already have and what we want." He looked at Lucille who, even in her working clothes, was beautiful. She had a smooth face framed by lustrous black hair, large dark eyes and a generous mouth. She radiated calmness, so that some of the villagers declared that she was the very image of the Mother of Christ, but to Challon she was just another woman to take, brutalise and discard. "Whatever we want," Challon said.

Sharpe said nothing and his face showed nothing. Lorcet, though, flinched at the sergeant's crudeness. "We only want the Emperor's gold," the lawyer said, his tone implicitly reproving Challon, "and of course this," he held up the ruby.

"That was part of Bonaparte's treasure," Sharpe said, "and it must be worth a cent or two."

"But it is not worth 40,000 francs," Lorcet observed. He carefully put the stone into a pocket of his waistcoat, then took from his bag a sheaf of papers, a pen and a bottle of ink. "You will write to this Monsieur Plaquet," he instructed Sharpe, pushing the pen and paper across the table, "introducing your good friend *Maître* Lorcet and saying that he is taking over the custody of the gold."

"Won't work," Sharpe said flatly, staring at the lawyer.

"It had better work!" Lorcet snapped, finally showing some impatience.

Sharpe sighed and shook his head. "I've got a wife, Lorcet," he said, "a thieving woman in England, and she stole all my money because I wrote my London banker a letter saying she could be trusted. So Monsieur Plaquet and I have an arrangement. He doesn't release any money except to me. Personally." He tapped his chest. "To me."

Lorcet glanced at Lucille who, startled because she knew none of these arrangements, nevertheless nodded. "It's true," she whispered, meaning it was true that Jane Sharpe had stolen her husband's money, though whether anything else Sharpe had said was true, she did not know.

"I have to go to the bank myself," Sharpe went on, "with my key. Otherwise? Nothing."

"So where is the key?" Lorcet demanded.

Sharpe glanced at a rack of keys hanging beside the kitchen door, Lorcet nodded permission, and Sharpe stood and took down a great black heavy key that looked as old as time, and Lucille at last began to understand that he was playing a game, for the key opened no vault in Caen, but instead unlocked the chateau's neglected chapel.

Sharpe tossed the key to the lawyer. "You get me and that key to Caen, Lorcet," he said, "and you get your money."

"How far is it to Caen?" Lorcet asked.

"Three hours by cart," Sharpe said, "and I'll have to take the cart, because 40,000 francs in gold weighs more than a ton. An hour to load the money, then three and a half hours back? Longer if it snows."

"Then pray it does not snow," Lorcet said, "for if you are not back by nightfall I shall assume you have betrayed us, and I shall let Sergeant Challon deal with your family." He paused, evidently expecting some reaction from Sharpe, but the Englishman's face showed nothing. "I shall regret that, Major," Lorcet said, "for I detest violence." He laid the key on the table. "Corporal Lebecque will accompany you with two men. If you attempt to summon help, Major, the corporal will kill you. But do as I ask, and we will all survive the day, though admittedly," he smiled thinly, "you will be somewhat poorer."

Sharpe picked up the key. "I'll be back here before nightfall," he promised the lawyer, then he stooped to kiss Lucille and his son.

Lucille clutched at him. "Richard!"

He eased her fingers from his coat collar. "Look after Patrick, love," he said, then kissed her again. "I'll be back," he whispered.

And he would be.

Corporal Lebecque and his two men watched as Sharpe harnessed the two horses. They were old horses, slow and heavy, who had spent most of their lives hauling French twelve pounder cannons, and now helped make Sharpe's life difficult because he had never liked or understood horses. Sharpe drew the reins back to the cart's box, but Lebecque would not trust him to drive, instead ordering one of his men to take the reins while Sharpe sat in the back of the cart where Lebecque lifted the skirts of his heavy coat to reveal a pistol. "I should have shot you in Naples," the corporal said.

"You were with Ducos when I came for the gold?" Sharpe asked. "I don't remember you."

"But I remember you," Lebecque said, then he shouted for the gate to be opened and the driver cracked the whip so that the heavy cart jolted forward. The first snow began to fall in big, loose flakes that melted as soon as they touched the road. The cart lurched from side to side, for Sharpe had deliberately mis-harnessed the horses. The bigger black horse had always been the offside leader on its team, while the chestnut had been harnessed behind the leaders, and Sharpe had put the offside leader on the wrong side and he had not tied the horses back by connecting the bit of each to the inside hame of the other, and that meant one horse could get in front and so slew the cart. None of the hussars had noticed, but they did sense something was wrong as the horse on the nearside kept trying to pull ahead and across its partner. The frustrated horse pulled like a pig and the driver slashed at it with the whip which only made it pull harder. "You have to rein in the black horse," Sharpe told the driver.

"I know how to drive," the man said, and the cart lurched again, almost throwing Lebecque clear across the cart.

"Curb the black," Sharpe said, "and let the chestnut set the pace."

"Shut your face," the man said, then cracked the whip again and the black horse jerked forward, the chestnut one baulked, and Lebecque and the other guard held on tight as the cart jolted up over the road's central ridge.

"Bastards!" Lebecque swore at the horses and the driver lashed down with the whip, and the two horses shoved at each other and the cart pitched again like a storm-tossed boat.

"I'm telling you!" Sharpe insisted, "let the chestnut lead!"

Lebecque swore as the cart bumped down again into the ruts. "Stop!" he shouted, and the driver obediently hauled on the reins. "You," Lebecque pointed at Sharpe, "you drive. And I'll be beside you with this." He lifted his coat to show the big pistol again.

Sharpe obediently climbed onto the box. Lebecque joined him there, while the other two men settled in the back. Those two men were also armed with pistols, but Sharpe now had them where he wanted them, just as he was where he wanted to be. He had escaped the farm and he was ready to fight back.

He clicked his tongue, curbed the black horse's speed, and let the cart climb the steady slope to the village. The snow was fitful and light, whirling in the black branches, but the sky was getting ominously darker and Sharpe reckoned the snow would soon be heavy and he also knew that a blizzard would never let him reach Caen and back in a day, but nor did he have any intention of going to Caen, for Monsieur Plaquet did not exist, nor was there any great iron-bound chest in a stone vault on the Rue Deauville. There was just a woman and a child to rescue, but for now Sharpe let the cart rumble along the village street where folk hurried towards the church for the Christmas Eve mass. Sharpe nodded to one or two acquaintances, then saw Jacques Malan standing in the doorway of the tavern. The big man had just been going into the inn when he saw Sharpe appear, but he waited in the cold long enough to spit into the roadway as Sharpe passed.

"*Bonjour*, Sergeant Malan," Sharpe said cordially, but Malan just ducked into the tavern and slammed the door. Sharpe hauled on the reins, turning the cart down the alley beside the inn.

"You don't use the main road?" Lebecque asked suspiciously.

"Short cut," Sharpe said. "Sooner we're done, sooner we're warm again."

"My God, it's cold," Lebecque grumbled. The corporal tugged his coat tighter about his thin body, and Sharpe knew the heavy coat would make it much harder for Lebecque to extricate the pistol. Sharpe was relying on that, but afterwards? God only knew how he would manage the rest.

The alley turned into a narrow lane that passed the butcher's yard and then ran downhill between high banks topped with hedges. At the bottom of the hill the road turned sharply east and then skirted a steep and wooded stream bank. Sharpe would normally have jumped off the box and walked the horses down the hill, but this day he let the cart's weight drive the beasts down the slope so they were going at a dangerously fast trot when they reached the bend above the stream.

"Careful!" Lebecque snapped.

"I drive here every day," Sharpe lied, and he cracked the whip hard and hauled on the reins so that the horses swerved around the corner and, just as Sharpe had expected, the cart's offside wheels caught in the deep ruts and the vehicle tipped towards the stream as it was dragged about the bend.

He heard the men behind shout as they were thrown across the cart, but he had already abandoned the whip and reins and seized one of Lebecque's pigtails. He threw himself forward off the box, hauling Lebecque with him as the cart rolled to the right. The frightened horses jerked to a halt as the half overturned cart cracked to a halt against a tree.

Lebecque and Sharpe had tumbled onto the splinter

bar behind the horses' legs and Sharpe, still holding the corporal's pigtail, thumped his left hand hard down onto Lebecque's throat. The corporal gasped for breath, Sharpe hit him on the Adam's apple again, then pulled Lebecque's coat aside to find the pistol, and the corporal, whose every breath was now like swallowing acid, was powerless to resist. Sharpe slammed the butt of the pistol into Lebecque's left temple, then scrambled over the tangle of traces and reins to find the two remaining men half down the stream's steep bank. One had struck his head against a tree as the cart capsized, and he was lying pale-faced on the grass, while the other man had been thrown into a thorn bush, where he was fumbling to free his pistol.

"Don't move," Sharpe said, and hauled back the pistol's cock.

"No, *monsieur*! Please!" the man said. The wheels of the upset cart were still turning.

"I do hate hussars," Sharpe said, walking up to the man. "Should have killed you all when I had the chance. I liked killing hussars." He straightened his arm, pointing the pistol.

"*Monsieur, non!*" The man thought he was about to be shot, but instead Sharpe uncocked the pistol, reversed it, and smacked the heavy butt hard against the hussar's skull. The man cried aloud, slumped down and Sharpe dragged him free of the thorn bush and then hit him again just to make sure he stayed quiet. He took the man's gun and then dealt with the third man who was already half stunned. "Three hussars against one rifleman," Sharpe said, "no wonder we won the bloody war. Lebecque! Stop croaking like a bloody frog and come here."

Sharpe still had the knife he had used to slice off the fox's brush and he used it to cut the reins into short lengths. He hated doing it. Harness was expensive, but he needed to tie the three men up and he had nothing else to hand, and so he sacrificed the leather. Once the men were secured he kicked them to their feet, tied them together with another length of rein, and then kicked them up the hill towards the village. The church bell, which had been tolling to call the faithful to mass, stopped. Snow sifted through the trees. It was falling more heavily now, settling on the hedgerows and in the ruts of the road. It was only mid-morning, but the clouds had turned the day into dusk.

So far, Sharpe thought, so good. He had freed himself and defeated half of Lorcet's small force, but that had been the easy part for a soldier like Sharpe. Now came the hard part. He was a rifleman and he was used to dealing with enemies, but now, instead, he would have to make some friends.

The goose that should have been Sharpe's Christmas dinner was now roasting in the oven, though the bird would take some hours to cook and Sergeant Challon was too hungry to wait, and so Lucille was frying eggs and bacon to feed the sergeant and one of his two hussars who had stayed in the farm. The second hussar was keeping guard on the gate-tower from where he could see both bridges across the chateau's moat, while Lorcet declared he did not like eggs and was content to breakfast on bread and an apple. "The flesh of animals," the lawyer declared, "thickens a man's blood. It makes him sluggish, so I eat nothing but fruit, vegetables and grains."

"I like thick blood," Sergeant Challon said as he walked to stand close behind Lucille. "So why are you married to an Englishman?" he demanded.

"We are not married," Lucille said, spooning hot fat onto the eggs.

"A Frenchman isn't good enough for you, eh?"

Lucille shrugged and did not answer. Lorcet frowned. He was seated at the table where he was trying to decipher Sharpe's account books. "Leave her alone," he told Challon.

The big man ignored the lawyer. "So what's wrong with a Frenchman?" he demanded of Lucille.

"The Englishman came here," Lucille said, "it is as

simple as that."

Challon put his arms around Lucille's waist, making her stiffen. "I think you're a traitor to France," the sergeant said, then slid one hand up to a breast. He smiled as he caressed her, then yelled and leaped away from the stove. "Bitch!" he snarled, clasping the hand where Lucille had spooned steaming fat onto his skin. He let go of the wounded hand so that he could hit Lucille, then went very still as he saw she was poised to throw the whole pan of eggs, bacon and sizzling fat into his face. Marie, who was cradling Patrick, laughed.

"Sit down, Sergeant," Lorcet said tiredly, "and leave her alone. You have more apples, Madame?"

"They are in the larder behind you," Lucille said, then carried the pan to the table where she tipped eggs and bacon onto one of the plates, but paused before giving any to Challon. "You owe me an apology, Sergeant," she said.

He was about the curse her, then saw that the pan was poised over his groin. "I apologise, Madame," he said grudgingly.

Lucille tipped the rest of the food onto his plate. "*Bon appetit,*" she said sweetly.

"So why *are* you with the Englishman?" the lawyer asked, bringing another apple from the rack in the larder.

"I told you," Lucille said, "he arrived here one day and he stayed."

"You allowed him to stay," Lorcet corrected her.

"That is true," Lucille conceded.

"An Englishman has no business in France," Lorcet said.

"His business," Lucille said, "is mending the mill, rearing lambs, raising cattle and tending the orchards. You want coffee?"

"Coffee excites the liver," Lorcet said disapprovingly, "and I refuse to touch it. But tell me, Madame, why an Englishman is mending your mill and tending the orchards. There are Frenchmen who could do that and who should be doing that. There's no work, *Madame*. These men," he indicated the two hussars who were eating as though they had not seen food in a month, "fought for France. They bled, they burned, they starved, they thirsted, and they came home to what? To a fat king on a fat throne and to rich folk in carriages, while they have nothing. Nothing!"

"So you let them steal?"

"Your Englishman stole our gold," Lorcet said. "I come merely to restore the gold to its rightful owners." He twisted and peered at the window. "Is it still snowing?"

"Harder than ever," Lucille said.

"Then pray your Englishman does not get stuck in a drift," Lorcet said.

Lucille smiled. "If I were you, *Maitre*," she said, using the formal address for the first time, "I would pray that he does get stuck." Lorcet frowned at her with incomprehension, and Lucille explained. "Because if he is stopped by the snow," she said, "he won't come back here. And then you might live."

"You terrify us," Sergeant Challon sneered at her.

"You sent only three men with him," Lucille pointed out calmly, then made the sign of the cross, "and I pray that their souls will rest in peace. But worry not, Sergeant. Major Sharpe will come back." A gust of wind rattled the door and Challon whipped round, his hand going to Sharpe's rifle that he had adopted as his own weapon. Lucille seemed amused at his alarm, then picked up some sewing. "My rifleman will come back, Sergeant," she said, "I promise you that. He will be back."

Father Defoy finished the mass with the blessing, then made his few announcements: tomorrow's mass would be an hour earlier, there would be no catechism class, and lastly a very public appeal to the widow Malan that she would remind her son that he had promised to deliver fuel to the priest's house and the promise had not been kept. Madame Malan stayed very straight-faced, though everyone in the church knew she was ashamed of

Jacques. He had been a good soldier, but now he was a wastrel and the widow did not know how she was to go on feeding him. Father Defoy was also worried about Jacques Malan, for the big man did nothing except cause trouble about the village. "You will remind him, Madame?" Father Defoy asked.

"I shall, father," Madame Malan answered.

"I can fetch the fuel, father," a man offered.

"I think Jacques should do something useful, don't you?" Father Defoy suggested, then looked alarmed because the church door had been thrown open. Wind gusted snow into the small church and flickered the candles burning in front of Mary's statue that had been wreathed by red-berried holly in honour of Christmas.

Three men, two of them with bloodied faces and all with tied hands, were thrust into the church and behind them came Monsieur Sharpe, the Englishman, carrying a huge pistol.

"Monsieur Sharpe!" Father Defoy remonstrated. "This is the house of God!"

"Sorry, Father," Sharpe said, pushing the pistol into a pocket of his coat and snatching off his snow-encrusted hat. "I've brought you three sinners who want to make confession." He kicked Corporal Lebecque up the aisle. "Three miserable sinners, Father, whose souls need shriving before I send them to hell."

"Monsieur Sharpe!" the priest protested again. "You left the door open!"

"So I did, Father," Sharpe said. The congregants were frowning at him, appalled by his apparent desecration of their church. Sharpe seemed oblivious of their disapproval as he pushed his three prisoners down to their knees in front of the pulpit. "Wait there, you scum," he said, then he turned back to the priest. "I left the door open, father," he explained, "because I stopped at the tavern on the way here and invited more of your parishioners to come to church."

Father Defoy had wondered whether Sharpe was drunk, but it was apparent he was not, and the priest rather liked the Englishman. He wished he came to church as Lucille did, but apart from that he had found Monsieur Sharpe to be straight-forward, tough, full of common sense and useful. It was a pity, of course, that the rest of the village did not share those opinions, but Jacques Malan had threatened to beat up anyone who offered the Englishman a welcome.

And now, to Father Defoy's surprise, Jacques Malan appeared in the church door, attended by a dozen cronies who had been ignoring the mass to drink apple brandy in the tavern. They had been carousing happily enough, content to let their mothers, wives or daughters look after God, when Sharpe had kicked the tavern door open and hauled a bloody-faced Corporal Lebecque into view.

"I've just kicked ten kinds of shit out of three hussars," Sharpe had announced belligerently to the tavern, "and if any of you want to know why, then come to the church now." He had said nothing more, but instead dragged his prisoner out of the doorway and the men, astonished and curious, had abandoned their drink to follow.

Jacques Malan pulled off his hat and made the sign of the cross, but kept good hold of the cudgel he always carried. He gave the priest a surly nod. "The Englishman wants trouble, father," he growled.

"No," Sharpe said, "I do not."

Father Defoy, fearing that the church was about to witness some unseemly violence, hurried forward to take charge of the situation, but Sharpe gestured the priest to silence. Then he looked at the villagers. "You don't like me, do you?" he challenged them. "You reckon I'm a stranger, an Englishman who spent most of his life fighting against Frenchmen, and now I'm here and you don't want me, do you?"

"No," Jacques Malan said, and his cronies grinned.

"But I want you," Sharpe said, "because where I come from neighbours help each other, and you're my neighbours now and I need help. So I've got a story to tell. A story about an Emperor and gold and greed. Do you want to hear it?"

"No!" Malan shouted, but the other villagers hushed him. They were mostly simple folk and they liked a good story, and they wanted to hear the tale and so Sharpe stood by his three cowed prisoners and he told the parishioners how the Emperor's gold had been stolen by Pierre Ducos, and how Ducos had arranged matters so that everyone believed Sharpe was the thief. "I needed to prove I was innocent," Sharpe said, "and Madame's brother, you remember Henri Lassan, God rest his soul? Of course you do. *Monsieur* Lassan knew something about Ducos, or I thought he did, and so I went to the Chateau Lassan to ask questions and do you know what happened? Madame shot me in the leg!"

Most of the villagers laughed at his indignation. Jacques Malan scowled, but even he was now listening as Sharpe, when the laughter ended, told them about Ducos, and how he had been called Major, but was not really a soldier at all. Pierre Ducos had been a *fonctionnaire,* he told them, and they sighed for they had all suffered greatly at the insolent hands of officials, and Ducos had also been a secret policeman, Sharpe added, and the black-shawled heads shook in horror of that indictment. "But there was worse," Sharpe said, embellishing the tale with a small untruth, "Monsieur Ducos was a lawyer!" Some of the women crossed themselves and, as Sharpe paused, there was an utter silence in the church.

"Monsieur Ducos stole the Emperor's gold," Sharpe said, "and I went to Naples to find him. And I killed him there and I took the gold back. Thousands and thousands of gold francs! The Emperor's lost gold!" The folk stared at him, transfixed, for there were few things closer to a peasant's heart than gold.

"But I did not travel to Naples alone," Sharpe said, and he took hold of Corporal Lebecque's collar. The villagers still did not know why Lebecque and his two companions were Sharpe's prisoners, and they watched wide-eyed as the hussar was dragged to his feet at the front of the aisle. "This man," Sharpe said, "was one of Ducos's companions. Isn't that true, Lebecque?"

Lebecque nodded.

"So you tell them, Corporal," Sharpe went on, "who came to Naples with me."

Lebecque's nose was running and his hands were tied behind his back, so all he could do was sniff. "Soldiers," he said miserably.

"What sort of soldiers?"

Lebecque paused, but Sharpe tightened his grip on the man's hair. "French soldiers," the corporal admitted.

"What sort of soldiers?" Sharpe asked.

"French!" Lebecque said louder.

Sharpe looked directly at Malan as he asked the next question. "And what uniform were they wearing, Corporal?"

Lebecque looked sullen, then shrugged. "The Imperial Guard," he said.

"Louder," Sharpe demanded. "Head up, man! Back straight! Let's hear you!"

Lebecque instinctively stood up straight. "They were from the Imperial Guard," he said, and Sharpe saw that Jacques Malan had heard the answer. He had wanted Jacques Malan to hear, for Malan had been an Imperial Guardsman himself and he still wore one of the great moustaches that Napoleon's hand picked warriors had sported.

"The Imperial Guard," Sharpe repeated, still staring at Malan, "and I fought alongside them. I fought under the orders of General Jean Calvet." He saw that name register on Malan's suspicious face. "And I was not fighting for Britain," Sharpe went on, "but for France. And when we had taken back the gold, we did not keep it. It went to Elba!"

That statement did not go down quite as well as he had hoped, for most of the villagers, far from being impressed by his honesty, plainly thought he was daft for having allowed such a fine treasure to escape.

"But these men," Sharpe indicated Lebecque and the other two prisoners, "believe I still possess the gold. So they came here. Six of them. And three are still in the chateau where they are holding Madame, our child and Marie as hostages." A murmur ran through the church. "And I have come here," Sharpe finished, "because you are my neighbours, and because I need your help." He pushed Lebecque back to the other prisoners, then turned to Father Defoy and shrugged as though he had nothing more to say.

There was silence in the church for a few seconds, then an urgent muttering. One man demanded to know why they should help Sharpe at all, and Sharpe spread his hands as if to suggest he could think of no good reason. "But you all know Madame," he said, "and Marie has lived here all her life. Would you abandon two of your women to these thieves?"

Father Defoy shook his head. "But we're not soldiers!" the priest said. "We should call the gendarmes from Caen!"

"If we can even get to Caen in this snow," Sharpe said, "and at nightfall," he continued, "Lucille will die while the gendarmes are still looking for their boots."

"But what do you want us to do?" another man asked plaintively.

"He wants us to fight his battles for him," Jacques Malan growled from the back of the small church, "because that's how the English fight. They let the Germans fight for them, the Spanish, the Portuguese, the Scots, the Irish, anyone but the English. The English don't fight, they let others suffer." A murmur of agreement sounded from Malan's supporters, then Malan looked momentarily alarmed as Sharpe strode down the aisle. The big man hefted his cudgel, but did nothing as Sharpe pushed past him.

"Outside," Sharpe said, pulling open the church

door.

"I don't obey you," Malan said stubbornly.

"Lost your courage, have you?" Sharpe sneered as he walked out into the snow. "All words, no action?"

Malan came through the door like a charging bull, only to find Sharpe sitting on the church's low wall. "Stand up," Malan demanded.

"Just get it over," Sharpe said, "hit me." He saw the puzzlement on Malan's face. "That's what you've been wanting to do all year, isn't it?" Sharpe asked. "Hit me? So do it."

"Stand up!" Malan said again, and his supporters, who had followed Malan out of the church, growled their support.

"I'm not going to fight you, Jacques," Sharpe said, "because I don't need to. I've been in as many battles as you have, so I don't have to prove a damned thing. But you do. You don't like me. In fact you don't seem to like anyone. You do nothing all day except make trouble. You were supposed to deliver firewood to the church house, weren't you? But you haven't done it because you'd rather sit in the tavern spending your mother's money. Why don't you make yourself useful? I could use you! I've got a rusted-up sluice gate that needs rebuilding, and a mill channel that needs clearing, and next month I've got a load of stone coming from Caen to repave the yard. I could do with a strong man, but right now I need a soldier. A good soldier, not some fat drunk who lives off his poor mother's purse."

Malan stepped forward and raised the cudgel. "Get up," he insisted.

"Why bother?" Sharpe asked, "if you're just going to knock me down again?"

"You're frightened!" Malan jeered.

"Of a drunk?" Sharpe asked scornfully.

"You dare call me a drunk?" Malan shouted. "You? The English? Who were always drunk in battle!"

"That"s true," Sharpe admitted, "but we had to be, didn't we? If we were going to fight you lot."

Malan blinked, unsure how to take Sharpe's agreement. "You were drunk?" he asked, sounding surprised.

"Not me, Sergeant Malan, not me. But a lot of the lads were. You can't blame them though, can you? They were terrified of the Imperial Guard. Best soldiers in Europe."

Jacques, wrongly assuming the last four words applied to the Imperial Guard, nodded. "We were," he said fervently, putting the cudgel onto his shoulder as though it were a musket.

"And you know what that makes you and me, Jacques?" Sharpe asked.

"What?" Malan asked suspiciously.

"The best soldiers in the village." Sharpe stood. "You and me, Jacques Malan, two of the very best there ever were. Real soldiers! Not like those hussars I dragged up here."

Malan shrugged. "Hussars!" He spat. "Girls on horseback."

"So what I'm saying, Jacques Malan, is help me or hit me."

"Hit him!" One of Malan's supporters shouted, then stepped back in alarm as Sharpe wheeled on him.

"Who are you to tell Sergeant Malan what to do?" Sharpe demanded. "He's a soldier, not a useless layabout. Him and me? We've seen war. Seen blood. Watched men scream. Seen the world on fire. Don't you dare give orders here, you worm."

Malan, flattered by Sharpe's words, frowned. "How do I help you, Englishman?" He still sounded wary, but in Sharpe's sudden anger he had seen a flash of the soldier Sharpe had once been and Malan liked soldiers. He missed their world.

"How do I get inside the chateau without them seeing me?" Sharpe asked. "They're bound to have a sentry in the tower, and there're only two bridges over the moat and that sentry can see both, but there has to be another way in."

"How would I know?" Malan said indignantly.

"Because you were sweet on Madame when you were young," Sharpe said, "and one day you got onto the chateau's roof to look through her bedroom window and you didn't get there by crossing either bridge, did you?"

Malan looked embarrassed, then decided the story did him some honour so he nodded. "There is a way," he admitted.

"So show me," Sharpe said, "and after that, if you really have to, you can hit me."

"That will be my pleasure," Malan said, but without any anger.

"But first," Sharpe said, "we have to organize the choir."

"The choir?"

"Watch me," Sharpe said. He clapped the big man on the shoulder. "I knew, from the moment when I was in trouble, that I needed you. Only you."

Malan was not quite sure how he had been talked round, but he was still pleased. "Me?" he asked, wanting the compliment repeated.

Sharpe obliged. "You're a soldier, Jacques. And I like soldiers." He took one of the captured pistols from his pocket and pushed it into Malan's hand. "You'll find that more useful than a cudgel, Jacques."

"I have my musket at home."

"Then fetch it. Then join me here. And…Sergeant?" Sharpe paused. "*Merci beaucoup*." He hid his sigh of relief, then went back into the church. He had a choir to organise.

S ergeant Challon finished off the last of the goose, patted his belly and leaned back in his chair. Lucille was putting Patrick to bed upstairs and Challon raised his eyes to the ceiling. "She can cook, that one," the sergeant said appreciatively.

"Goose is harmful to the nerves," the lawyer maintained. "Too rich, too fatty. You should avoid it above all other meats." He had almost finished with Sharpe's accounts and was wondering why there was no evidence of the stolen gold in the columns. Probably, he thought, because the Englishman had wanted to keep the plunder a secret.

"I could eat another goose," Challon grunted, then looked at the lawyer. "So what will you do with the woman when her Englishman gets back?"

The lawyer drew a finger across his throat. "It's for the best, sadly" he said. "I detest violence, but if we let them live they'll only tell the gendarmes. And Major Ducos's will is hardly clear title to the gold, is it? The Government will want it. No, we have to make certain that Major Sharpe and his woman do not talk."

"So if the woman's going to die," Challon said, "does it matter when? Or what happens to her first?"

Lorcet frowned. "I find your suggestion distasteful, Sergeant,"

Challon laughed. "You can find it what you like, *Maître*, but she and I have got some unfinished business." He pushed back his chair.

"Sergeant!" Lorcet snapped, then found himself staring into the blackened muzzle of Challon's pistol.

"Be careful, lawyer," the sergeant said. "You've brought us to the gold, and you say you'll pay us well, but what's to stop us taking it all?"

Lorcet said nothing. Challon holstered the pistol, smiled and went out of the room. His boots were loud on the wooden stairs. He saw candlelight coming from the room at the end of the upper corridor and he pushed through the door to see Lucille and Marie fussing over the baby they had put into a crib at the end of the bed. "You," Challon pointed at Marie, "downstairs!"

"*Non, monsieur!*" Marie said, then gasped as the sergeant took hold of her dress, pulled her roughly to the door and kicked her out into the passage. "Downstairs!"

he snarled at her, then slammed the door shut and turned to Lucille. "Madame," he said, "you are about to enter paradise."

But before Challon could move there was a sudden rush of feet in the passage and the man who had been keeping watch from the tower ran into the bedroom. His greatcoat was thick with unmelted snow and there was a look of alarm on his face. "Sergeant!"

"What is it?"

"People! Scores of them! Coming here."

Challon swore and hurried after the man towards the tower. They had to go out into the yard, that now had an inch or more of new snow, then into the gate tower, up the stairs and through the hatch which led to the ancient rampart which overlooked the moat's front bridge. And from there Challon could see a crowd of people walking slowly down the hill towards the chateau. "What in God's name is that?" he asked, because the man leading the procession was a priest dressed in full vestments and behind him a cloaked man carried a silver crucifix on a tall pole. The priest made no attempt to cross the bridge and demand admittance through the big gate, instead he arrayed his parishioners on the road that edged the moat at the front of the chateau. "Stay here," Challon ordered the sentry, then went back to the kitchen where he dragged Lorcet from the account books and took him into the front parlour from where they could see the priest and his flock beyond the moat.

"What're they doing?" Lorcet asked.

"God knows," Challon said. He was still holding Sharpe's rifle, but what was he to do? Shoot the priest?

"Are they going to sing?" the lawyer asked incredulously, for the priest had turned to his flock, raised his hands, and now brought them down. And so the crowd began to sing.

They sang carols in the falling snow. They sang all the beautiful old hymns of Christmas, the songs of a baby and a star, of a manger and shepherds, of a virgin birth and of angels' wings beating in the winter sky over Bethlehem. They sang of wise men and of gold, of peace on earth and joy in heaven. They sang lustily, as though the loudness of their voices could stave off the bitter cold of the waning afternoon.

"In a moment," Lucille had come down from the bedrooms, "they will want to come in and I must give them wine and food."

"They can't come in!" Lorcet snapped.

"How will you stop them?" Lucille asked as she folded Patrick's clothes onto the parlour table. "They know we're here. We have lamps shining."

"You will tell them to go away, Madame!" Lorcet insisted.

"Me!" Lucille asked, her eyes widening. "I should tell my neighbours that they cannot sing me carols on Christmas Eve? *Non, monsieur*, I shall not tell them any such thing."

"Then we'll just leave the doors locked," Sergeant Challon decided, "and they can freeze to death. They'll get tired soon enough. And you, Madame, had better pray that your Englishman is bringing the gold."

Lucille went back to the stairs. "I shall pray, Sergeant," she assured Challon, "but not for that." She went up to her child.

"Bitch," Challon said, and followed her. While outside the carollers sang on.

"There used to be a third bridge over the moat," Jacques Malan explained, "and it led to the chapel, but they pulled it down years ago. Only they left the stone pilings, see? Left them just under the water."

Malan had not only fetched his musket, but had put on his old uniform so that now he was glorious in the blue, white and scarlet of Napoleon's old guard, though the waistcoat and jacket no longer could be buttoned over his spreading belly. Still, he looked fine in the uniform and, thus dressed for battle, he had led Sharpe on a wide circuit through the woods so that they approached the chateau from the east, hidden from the gate-tower by the farmhouse and the chapel roof.

Malan now reversed his musket and stabbed its stock down through the moat's skim of ice. "There," he said, as the musket butt struck stone. He stepped carefully across so that he was standing on the piling with two inches of water lapping his boots. He probed for the next stone. "There are five pilings altogether," he told Sharpe. "Miss one, though, and you'll fall in the water."

"But what happens once we're across?" Sharpe asked, for the vanished bridge led to nothing but a blank stone wall.

"We climb to the roof," Malan said. "There's a stone jutting out, see?" He pointed. "We throw a rope round it and climb."

And once they were on the chapel roof, Sharpe thought, there was a window into an old attic that was filled with eight hundred years of junk, and the attic led through to the main house where there was a hatch into the big bedroom. He had only ever been into the attic once and he had marvelled at the collection of rubbish that Lucille's family had stowed away. There was a complete suit of armour up there and crates of mouldering clothes, ancient arrows, a crossbow, a weathercock which had fallen from the chapel's gable, a stuffed pike caught by Lucille's grandfather and a rocking horse that Sharpe thought he might get down for Patrick, though he hoped the toy would not put the idea of becoming a cavalryman into the boy's head.

"I'd never live that down," he said out loud.

"Live what down?" Malan asked. He was standing on the third hidden piling, and probing for the fourth.

"If Patrick becomes a cavalryman."

"*Mon Dieu*! That would be terrible!" Malan agreed, then jumped across the last stones and onto the narrow ledge that edged the chapel. He held out his musket to help Sharpe across the last two pilings. "They sing well!" he said, listening to the choir of villagers. "You do this carol singing in England, too?"

"Of course we do."

"But my captain said the English did not believe in God."

"But they do believe in getting free food and drink," Sharpe said.

"So maybe they're not so mad after all," Malan conceded. "And you have brandy in the house, monsieur? Not that I am a drunk, of course."

"I have good brandy," Sharpe said, then watched as Malan fetched a length of rope from a pocket of his guardsman's coat. "I'll go first," Sharpe said.

"You will follow me!" Malan insisted, as he tossed the rope to loop it over the projecting stone. "I have done this before. You hold the musket."

Malan was surprisingly nimble for a big man, though he was breathless by the time he reached the chapel roof. "I used to be able to do that in seconds," he grumbled.

"I thought you only did it once?" Sharpe said.

"Mademoiselle Lucille only saw me once," Malan corrected Sharpe. "Give me the musket barrel, monsieur, and I'll pull you up."

He caught hold of the barrel and, with an enviable ease, hauled Sharpe up onto the roof. "Now what?" he asked.

"The window," Sharpe said, pointing to the small, blackened panes of the old attic window that was set into the higher gable next to the slippery, snow-covered roof on which they were precariously perched. "Break it in."

"They'll hear us!"

"The choir is singing fit to burst their lungs," Sharpe said. "Why else do you think I asked them to come? So break the window. It'll be something else for you to mend."

"And what makes you think I'll be working for

you, Englishman?"

"Because I'll pay you," Sharpe said, "because you like Lucille and because you'd rather work for another soldier than sweat for some bastard who stayed at home while you went to war."

Malan grunted, but said nothing in response. Instead he used the musket's butt to push in the window panes, then he snapped out the old rotten mullions and struggled through into the attic. Sharpe followed him, relieved to be out of the snow. "Now follow me," he whispered, "and go gently! This place is full of rubbish."

It took a few moments to edge through the dusty, dark clutter, but at last Sharpe pushed the stuffed pike aside and crouched beside the old hatch. He put an ear to the wood, listened for a second, then angrily pulled the pistol from his coat pocket. "Let's go to war," he said to Malan, then pulled the hatch cover back.

L ucille screamed when Sergeant Challon shoved her down onto the bed. She had thought she would be safe now the villagers were outside the chateau, but the big sergeant had followed her upstairs and now he pushed her onto the big counterpane. Patrick cried, but there was nothing Lucille could do.

The choir sang of angels coming to earth. Lucille was sure Richard had somehow persuaded them to be there, though what else he might have arranged she did not know, but now she feared she would never find out for Sergeant Challon had peeled off his jacket and was unbuttoning the straps of his old hussar breeches. "You burned me!" he snarled at her, then paused in his undressing to slap her face with his burned hand. "Bitch!"

Lucille tried to scramble off the bed, then froze as Challon pointed his pistol between her eyes. He smiled when he saw her fear, then he tucked the pistol under his arm and began pulling down his breeches. "The Emperor gave us lots of practice with the ladies," he said. "Italian skirts, Spanish skirts, Portuguese skirts, we hauled them all up. So get yourself ready. I ain't a man who likes to be kept waiting."

The noise of the hatch opening made Challon look up at the ceiling, but he had no time to pluck the pistol from under his arm before Sharpe's boots raked down his face. Challon twisted away, falling under the impact, and his breeches were round his ankles and so he could not get to his feet, and then the Englishman was kneeling on his chest with one hand stifling his mouth and the other holding a pistol at his neck. The Englishman smiled then and Challon felt a shudder of fear.

"Get up," Sharpe said quietly, moving off Challon, and the sergeant was hauled to his feet and saw, right in front of him, a sergeant of the Imperial Guard with a most unfriendly face.

"Hold him, Major," Malan said.

Sharpe held Challon tight, Malan grinned, then kicked the hussar between the legs.

"Jesus!" Sharpe said in awe, as he let Challon fall. "He won't walk for a month!" He grinned at Lucille who had snatched up Patrick. "Where's Marie?" he asked.

"Safe," she said, "in her bedroom."

"And you're safe now," Sharpe said, then gestured at Jacques. "You know Sergeant Malan, of course."

"I am very glad to see you, Jacques," Lucille said fervently.

"*Madame*," Malan said gallantly, brushing at his moustache and then offering her a clumsy bow.

"What's going on up there?" *Maître* Lorcet shouted from the bottom of the stairs. He had heard the thump of Sharpe jumping on Challon, and the bigger thump as Malan followed, and he wondered just what injuries Challon was inflicting on the woman. "What're you doing?"

Sharpe opened the door. "Lorcet?" he called, "this is Major Sharpe. I've got four of your men prisoner, I've got my woman back, I've got my child, I've got an Imperial Guardsman who wants to murder someone, and there never was any gold. And right now I'm coming down the stairs and you can have a fight if you want one, but if you want to live then put the ruby on the table and sit down like a good little lawyer."

Jacques Malan dragged the whimpering Challon down the stairs and Sharpe locked the sergeant, Lorcet and the remaining hussar inside the unused chapel. They could repent of their sins there until morning when Sharpe would deal with them, but for now he had more important tasks. He sent Jacques to unlock the gate while he lit the fire in the big hall, for the folks who had been singing were all chilled to the bone.

So he lit the fire, then he and Jacques Malan went down to the cellar and hauled up dusty bottles that had been stored there since before the Revolution, and Sharpe, listening to the laughter, and wondering how Lucille had managed to find so much food in the house, reckoned he was staying in Normandy after all. It was Christmas, he had neighbours at last, and he was home.